Tales of the Fall
Book II

The Right Hand Path

J.A. Wynn

A MediaCrash Book

Published by MediaCrash Books

PUBLISHER'S NOTE
This is a work of fiction. Names, characters, places, and incidents either are the product of the author's imagination or are used fictitiously, and any resemblance to actual persons, living or dead, events, or locales is entirely coincidental.

Library of Congress Catalog Card Number: PENDING

ISBN: 978-0-9821837-2-4

First Edition: July 2016

1 2 3 4 5 6 7 8 9 10 IN 20 19 18 17 16

Contents

CONTENTS

The Fifth Tale

Outcasts, together

Chapter 1

The Traveler Awakens

Of the unfolding story
and of the continuing curse

THE SILENCE of the early morning was broken by the chattering of songbirds; the innkeeper came out from his rooms behind the tavern. Pulling a much-worn key from his vest pocket, he opened the door into the kitchen and entered the inn. He had just begun preparing for the day's work when he heard a loud thumping at the front door.

Muttering to himself about the hour, and wondering who would be banging at the door of a tavern just after dawn, he shuffled to the door and flung it open testily.

"What business do you have here, at such a wee hour?" he exclaimed. He was shocked to see men that he knew from the nearby village. "What do you all want?"

"We want to hear more from that one that was tellin' the tales last evening," began the leader of the group. "How does it all end?"

The rest nodded their agreement and shouldered past the innkeeper to fill the tables and bar. The innkeeper looked about in amazement as nearly every member of the small village filed into the room.

"But he's not about yet. I'm sure he's still asleep in his roo—" He swallowed the sentence as he saw the gathered villagers look beyond his shoulder at the stairs behind him. He turned to see the traveler descending. He was about to apologize when the traveler held up his hand, looking much the same as he'd looked the night before. The innkeeper knew what a well rested customer looked like; he suspected that the traveler had been awake the whole night and had heard the knocking at the door, just as he had.

"So, you want to hear more about the children, Mara and Solomon Worth?" the traveler asked in a low voice. The villagers murmured their assent.

"Very well," began the traveler, "Someone light a fire, and bring beer for the men and cider for the others. When we've broken our fast and settled in, I'll carry on with the story."

The innkeeper nodded and waved his arm to his wife and children. They had heard the commotion of so many boots on the floor of the inn and were hovering near the kitchen doorway. They scurried into the kitchen and started the breakfast. A few of the villagers hastened away to bring more food and drink, and a few others went to the kitchen to help. Before long, the fire was roaring, the breakfast was served and eaten, and the beer and cider were being passed around.

The traveler took the same chair that he'd sat in the night before and cleared his throat. The villagers quieted to a soft murmur as he looked over their faces. He softly began to speak.

"To tell the next part of the tale, I feel I must begin with Anomalie. Anomalie Harper..."

Chapter 2

Breakout

*Of the escape from the Old Zone
and of Anomalie's first blood*

WHEN Anomalie woke up, stretching and rubbing her sore muscles, she couldn't find the last moment of yesterday. It had slipped away in the night, flitted away into her dreams and hidden, forgotten in her weariness. She felt cheated, as if some other girl had stolen into her slumber and pilfered her thoughts and taken away her memory.

She wanted to remember what she'd felt before she drifted off. Before she had let her eyes fall, she had finally felt as if she had some direction, as if she had belonged. She felt as though she might be missed by someone at least, and she had never felt that way before. She glanced about and saw the other two lying next to her, dug into a slight depression in the sand outside the Old Zone, and the feeling came rushing back. The little girl slept soundly. Just beyond her was the man in gray. A small smile began to grow on Anomalie's face but she was startled slightly when she saw that his eyes were open, he was awake and staring at the fading stars. Quickly regaining her composure, she scowled to hide her discomfort.

"'morning," she said, looking away, "were you up all night?" Sigil turned his head towards where she was sitting on her haunches and focused on her.

"I slept a bit in the early part of the night. I sensed no danger." He sat up. "I sense none now." He rose, pulled himself out of the sleeping trench and began to break camp, casting about the edge of the site slowly and looking in all directions. "I saw that you slept at least. We must be moving soon but we will let the child sleep a bit more." He moved his head, gesturing to her to move away from Mara.

They had been hiking along the edge of the Old Zone for two days, dodging the Judicial patrols and drones, moving mostly at night except for short bursts when Sigil had determined that it was safe. Anomalie marveled at the gray man's ability to detect the Judicials. It was as though he had eyes that saw in every direction and ears like a fox. Her own sensors confirmed what he claimed but usually a moment too late. Little Mara seemed content to walk when they walked; she never seemed to show any sign of fatigue or frustration. Anomalie was certain that she had never seen a child so resilient.

The sun was beaming with a reddish tinge through the morning haze when Mara awoke. They ate a hasty breakfast of Sigil's fading military rations and chocolate that Anomalie had pilfered from home and, after cleaning the campsite, they shouldered their packs. Sigil looked expectantly at Anomalie.

"Where to from here?" he asked. Most of their journey had been through the rubble and piles of earth that surrounded the fenceline, but now Anomalie pointed away from the Old Zone, toward the open expanse that stretched to the horizon beneath the rising sun.

"We should be near the center point of the eastern fenceline, at least according to my GPS," she replied. "The Crax lie due east from here, across the Barrens."

"There is no road?" he asked as he bent and checked Mara's pack for her, insuring that there were no hanging straps and that Brownie was tucked safely inside with only his head protruding.

She laughed, "Hell no. There really is nothing between grids. The Judicials do their best to maintain resupply for each grid from the air. They mostly use drones. I guess they figure that it's not a good idea for us to travel much," she added sardonically. "I've never even been outside grid 4649, except to sneak into the Zone, and that's not really much of a grid at all."

He nodded, understanding. His brow furrowed in concentration, he shaded his eyes from the sun as he looked that way. "How far to the east are we walking?" he asked.

"I figure that it's only about two kilometers, but we can't walk it during the day. There's no cover out there. It's just blasted dirt. They used to send garbage crews out into the Barrens to pick it clean for metals. We should wait for nightfall again and—"

Sigil cut her off. "We have to get there before nightfall..." He paused, noticing what she had said, "Two klicks isn't far..." he stopped again, thinking. "I have an idea."

Anomalie glanced at him quizzically. "What do you have in mind?"

He gestured to the fenceline that surrounded the Old Zone. "Is there a way that we can get back inside there?" he asked. Anomalie blew a loose strand of hair away from her eyes; her lips bunched in dismay and she looked shocked that he would even suggest such a thing.

"Why would we want to go inside?" She turned her head and looked back toward the east. "We want to go that way." She waved her hand in the direction of the Crax. Sigil moved impatiently, motioning to Mara to follow him as he began to inspect the fence. They started to drift along it and Anomalie followed, wondering what they were looking for but hurrying to keep up. "I don't really know the east side. It's not like I hang out here."

After a time, the ground began to dip where a deep trench had been dug into the earth near the fence. They clambered down the incline and Sigil stopped and crouched where the fence met the ground. "Here," he said and pointed. Anomalie looked where he was pointing. Whatever mass had impacted the ground there had done more than just torn a hole in the ground. It had separated some of the fence, leaving a small gap.

"We can get in here, I think I can fit too," murmured Sigil. "We've got to hurry before the next patrol passes." They hastily pushed themselves through the gap, Anomalie first, turning to help Mara through and finally Sigil. When they were inside, they quickly moved deeper into the Zone and away from the fence. Further inside the Old Zone, the cracked concrete of the remnants of buildings provided them with a place to wait in hiding. They moved behind a low wall, shielding themselves from view and sat.

"What are we doing in here?" Anomalie asked when they had settled. Mara turned her head and studied the streets that were visible, splayed out into the Old Zone like cracked, skeletal fingers.

"We want a vehicle. Anything that seems to be still intact," Sigil answered. "I saw some hulks of things that looked like armor when we passed out of the Zone the first time."

Anomalie shook her head. "That stuff is crazy old though. There's no way that it can still work. Dumb idea."

He grinned at her in reply. "Not so dumb. This area was smashed with a nuclear exchange, contaminated. In the armor hunting business, that's not what we call a 'catastrophic kill'. There's no reason to think that every one of them has engine damage. I'm willing to hope that there could even be fuel intact."

She gaped at him when she realized that he was serious. Then, a thought came to her. "Like you said, this place is roasting with rads. Aren't you worried that the two of you could be cooked?" She looked nervously at Mara. "I've read that in your time radiation was much lower. People got sick from rads, right?" She didn't want Mara to get sick. Anomalie thought that the little girl was adorable. Thinking of her with radiation sickness was horrible.

Sigil shook his head. "Don't worry about it. Both of us are…" he paused. "Evolved, I guess you could say. Radiologically speaking." She looked at him skeptically. He went on. "You might say that we're emitting ourselves. But slightly out of phase." When he said that, he smiled slightly, as if he was laughing at his own private joke. He reached over and rumpled Mara's hair. She smiled back. He shifted his pack on his shoulders and spoke again. "We should begin searching now. We want to find what we're looking for before tonight. We'll hide out at the vehicle's location."

Anomalie held up a hand to stop him. "I can find what you're looking for. I can probably get some sat images of the Zone. Just take a sec'." Her eyes seemed to lose focus for an instant as she accessed her uplink. In a moment, she was scrolling through images in her heads-up display. When she found what she was looking for, she increased the resolution. "Is this good?" she asked. It seemed as if an image grew out of the air in front of her. She reached out with her hand, and with a swipe, spun it so that Sigil could see it. It shimmered as he peered at it. He moved his head closer and, with a static crack, it flickered and disappeared. "Sorry," she said, "interference from the loony radio junk in the air around here."

He nodded. "I saw what I needed to see. Rammers. Those will do fine. What direction are they from here?"

She pointed to the shattered street before them. "About 600 meters in that direction, and then to the left."

He dipped his head at her with an approving note in his eyes. She blushed. "Well then," he said, and stood. Mara stood at his side. "Let's get to it."

Keeping closely to the sides of the street, they managed to avoid any detection. Anomalie knew the Old Zone's quirks and they made it to their goal quickly. Sigil made a low whistle when he saw the vehicles.

"These are Rammers, pretty ancient tech. But they will do." He trotted toward the first vehicle eagerly. "Stand watch while I check them," he muttered. Anomalie nodded, crouched down and pulled Mara closer behind her. The four vehicles were along the edges of a foundation left in the ground where a building had once stood. One Rammer was toppled halfway into the hole, held tenuously aloft by a steel cobweb of rebar and cement chunks. The other three were still above ground. One was clearly destroyed, its armored shell torn away on one side. Something small had entered from below and to the right, punching a fist sized hole through the thinner armor near the ground. It had exited at the top and to the left, blowing the heavier armor outward and upward like a torn open tuna can. The remaining two looked to be intact and Sigil focused on one first. The Rammer was literally built like a tank, but had eight rubberine wheels that were nearly as tall as Anomalie. There was no large main gun, but instead there was a turret atop the hull from which two thick gun barrels protruded. He crawled underneath it and inspected it closely. Then he rolled out on one side and found the hatch. He opened it.

Inside there were four crew members, dressed in rotting jumpsuits, their nearly mummified bodies still at their combat stations. He ducked his head and climbed inside. After pulling the driver from his seat, he sat and looked closely at the controls. He reached for a start button, pressed it and a slight humming noise came from beneath the control panel. He smiled and lifted himself from the seat. Crouching down on all fours, he rolled onto his side next to the driver's seat and twisted a small latch that held the forward engine panel shut. The panel was stuck fast; he hammered it with the side of his fist and it stubbornly came loose. He peered inside, then reached back with his hand and pressed the start button again while he maneuvered some cables. A loud clicking erupted from the engine, causing Anomalie to startle. Pulling Mara closer, she glanced over her shoulder with a worried expression. Sigil tried again. This time, the motor came alive and the interior of the vehicle flooded with light. He quickly killed the motor, replaced the panel and crawled backwards. He pulled the crew members from the vehicle and tossed their bodies into the foundation hole. Then he walked to the back of the vehicle and signaled to Anomalie and Mara. Both girls stood and walked around to the hatch. Sigil motioned them inside and they sat in the darkened compartment.

"We'll wait here until nearly dark. In the meantime, I'll pull some other parts and gear from the other vehicles. If all goes well, we won't be noticed," he said.

They sat in the vehicle, the only illumination coming from Anomalie's heads-up projection. She maintained a dim glow so that Mara wouldn't be afraid of the dark, but the tiny girl appeared to be less nervous than she was. As the morning passed, Sigil pulled the power source and some other supplies from the other vehicle. One time, he came back lugging two large ammo cans. He stepped inside the compartment and moved to the rear. He located three other full cans there.

"We have quite a bit of ammunition, both for my rifle and the coaxial gun up top. It should last us a while." He opened one can and pulled out a belt of linked together bullets. "Hopefully," he added.

While they waited, Anomalie tried to get to know Mara. She was fascinated by her calmness, and remembered what Sigil had mentioned about her importance. She spoke tentatively to her, noticing her stuffed bear. "Have you two been friends long?" she started. "He seems like a nice bear. Cute." She ignored the ragged paw where the fur had worn off.

"He stayed with me the whole time when I was sick," Mara answered, smoothing the bear's fur and rearranging his position in her backpack. "I was sick for a long time."

Anomalie didn't want to bring up a bad memory for her, she looked fragile enough as it was. But, she couldn't overcome her curiosity.

"You don't seem sick now," she began gently. "You look all better now. What happened?"

"I was dead," said Mara. Anomalie nearly choked. She swallowed and was about to speak but the little girl went on, "Sigil brought me back to life."

Anomalie glanced over at Sigil. He had removed the larger gun from the turret and was working the bolt back and forth while spraying oil on it from a bottle he had found in a tool bag. She had about a million questions whirling through her head, but she couldn't pick one to begin with. So she went silent instead. She brought her attention back to her own view of her HUD and continued monitoring the street outside. While she adjusted her sensors, she also began to search through history files for any mention of someone named Sigil or Mara. She was good at multitasking, and ignoring things that were too troublesome to understand. She figured she would just find data about it later.

"Are you a robot?" asked Mara. "Sigil said you were a robot."

Anomalie grinned. "Not really. Robot is a bad word where I come from..." she answered. "Or when I come from I guess. The technical term for me is 'transhuman', because I have bionics inside of me. Or 'cyborg' maybe. Although that's not really accurate, people like using it. That's what people from your time would call me. But I prefer 'cyberpunk', I learned that word from vids and stuff that I found from your time. My favorite stuff..." she trailed off.

"I had a toy robot," Mara went on. "His name was Cogsley, and he could clap his hands and sing and say my name. He was cool. But I broke him," she finished sadly.

Anomalie grimaced as she checked out some movement on the street. It turned out to be only a torn piece of rag blowing in the dusty wind of the Zone. "I'm broken too," she said. "And I'm not really a great singer. Most of my silicon is only second or third gen." As if to emphasize her point, the light that she was providing for Mara flickered and dimmed. "Sorry, I get lots of artifacts in my datafeed. Plus, I have to crack into feeds that everybody else has full access to. Just because I have outdated crypticates." She sighed as the light came back to full intensity. "I have to crack nearly everything I read."

"What's a crypticate?" Mara asked.

"It's total bullsh—" Anomalie caught herself, glancing down at Mara's upturned eyes. "It's this annoying thing that's like a lock on information. Like a lock on books." Anomalie was struggling to find a point of reference for a conversation with a six year old from nearly two centuries before her time.

"We can open locks," replied Mara. "Any lock. Sigil is really fast too. St. Dismas said that a lock was meant to be—"

"Hush, Mara," interjected Sigil in a low voice. He held up a hand and Mara obediently became quiet. Anomalie saw what he saw. A Judicial patrol had turned the corner near the vehicles. Bunched up, the lead element was only a meter or so in front of a main force of about thirty Judicial Rangers. Anomalie quickly switched off her sensors, hoping that the patrol's scans had been too slow to spot her in the thick radio interference of the Old Zone. Sigil peered through the view port to the left of the gunner's seat, dropped silently down into the compartment and slid into the driver's seat. "Strap Mara into her seat," he whispered. "And strap down the packs."

Anomalie's heart bounced into her throat. In the corner of her eye, in the interface of her HUD, she saw a tiny level meter peak into a red blip as her heart rate began to rise. She took a few deep breaths and watched the meter settle down. First, she wrapped the pack straps around the bottoms of the chairs and cinched them tight, then she started to strap herself into one of the chairs but she saw Sigil look at her over his shoulder and shake his head. He pointed to the gun turret that he had just vacated.

"You. Up there." She gaped at him, but saw that he meant it. "The gun is ready. Don't touch the bolt. Just wait until we move and then grab the handles. Don't touch the triggers until I say." He reached his hand down and held it over the start button. "The turret is on a swivel and motorized. Just swing the gun and the turret will keep up." She pushed herself out of the chair and moved to the little ladder that went up to the gunner's seat. She closed her eyes briefly and then climbed up. The little meter in the corner of her eye was now fully red. She had never fired a gun before. She settled into the seat and looked at the trigger handles. They attached to a large metal box with a circular sight atop it. To one side, she saw the linked bullets stretching out and down into one of the ammo cans that Sigil had brought up. Each bullet looked thicker than her thumb and as long as her hand, with a vicious looking red tip on the end. She looked through the gunner's port and saw the twin barrels of the gun, stretching out and away from it, and she saw another circular sight at the end. Beyond that, she saw a group of Judicial Rangers gathered around a crouching ranger, a radio antennae poking from his back. One ranger stood with a mouthpiece to his head, with a short cord spiraling into the radioman's transmitter. She saw dull black and gray armor shifting on his shoulders and chest. Wiping the sweat from her hands on her pants leg, she glanced away from the gun sight to view the semi-transparent view of her HUD, scrolling through and selecting a song from a list of tracks. She picked "I Against I" by the Bad Brains and started it playing.

"Are you ready?" Sigil mouthed, looking up at her. There was a look of determination tinged with sadness on his face. She sucked in a breath and nodded. She grabbed the handles and lined up the front sight with the ranger with the mouthpiece. A grinding shriek sounded in her ears as the turret servo came to life and the rear sight lined up with the front sight. As the music swelled in her ears, she felt her seat shift with the turret and saw all three objects as one, the ranger, the front sight and the rear sight. The rangers' heads jerked around at the sound, staring at the Rammer. Sigil punched his hand down onto the start button and the compartment was filled with red light as the Rammer roared to life. She squeezed the triggers with both hands. There was a roaring flash at the ends of the barrels and she lost sight of the ranger and the radioman for a moment. The Rammer lurched forward and up over a pile of rubble, spitting rocks and debris behind it. The knobby tires skidded against the cracked concrete and then grabbed tightly as the vehicle shot toward the patrol, like a rabbit released from a trap. Anomalie saw smoke and then the rooftop of a building and, when her sights came down again, she saw nothing but a hole in the ground where the radioman had been crouching. There were also a few reddish chunks scattered around the hole but nothing that resembled the two rangers that had been there a moment before. She swung the gun around in a crazy arc, searching for the rest of the patrol, and she saw three rangers running toward the corner of the street and the safety of the building. She pushed up on the handles so that the barrels would depress and she saw the sights line up on the rangers as they fell into line behind each other. This time, she saw through the flash of light as her bullets found the mark. The rounds thudded into the nearest ranger, throwing him forward into the man in front of him. Then he flew apart as the next rounds impacted and all three rangers disintegrated into small pieces. Some of the bullets hit the side of the building beyond them and blew head sized chunks of concrete out of the wall. Before she could release the triggers, a man sized hole had been carved out of the corner of the building, leaving strings of steel reinforcement exposed. The Rammer raced past the last members of the patrol and skidded to the right around the corner. Sigil wrestled with the controls as the rear of the Rammer fishtailed onto the next street and hurtled toward the fenceline and the open space of the Barrens beyond.

Chapter 3

Beyond the Grids

Of the killing of a Drone
and of how they were collected

A NOMALIE had felt like an egg in a blender when they took the corner. She saw her HUD lose color and then crackle out of sight. Rubbing her shoulder where it had smashed into the side of the turret, she leaned back so that she could look down to where Mara sat. Although Mara was clutching Brownie tightly in her hands, there was an energetic grin spread across her face. She looked back at Anomalie and the older girl shared the smile.

"Owwww..." Anomalie yelled over the music pounding in her ears, directed specifically at Sigil. "That hurt you know. I'm not entirely made of titanium alloy. Just a few bits and pieces." Sigil answered by pushing the accelerator down hard with his foot, causing the Rammer's engine to whine. Anomalie was pushed backwards against the rear of the turret and her next words caught in her throat. She threw a dirty look his way as her HUD flickered back into sight. She heard clanging sounds and realized that they were bullets ricocheting off the rear armor of the Rammer. "I hope this armor holds up..." she shouted into the compartment.

Sigil didn't answer her but instead focused his attention on the street directly in front of the speeding Rammer. Anomalie swung the gun around to the front and looked through her gun port. The fence seemed to grow in size as they careened toward it; Anomalie couldn't believe how fast they'd covered 600 meters. She cranked the gun hard to the right and the motor whirred. The turret spun 180 degrees and she saw the street spin into view again. She saw a few flashes from where the remaining patrol members were firing at the rapidly escaping Rammer. She squeezed the triggers and watched the flashes stop as the rangers dove for deeper cover. She giggled, with a slightly manic grin. She spun the turret back to the front just as the Rammer crashed through the fence.

The front set of wheels cleared most of the trench that they had entered through but clipped the far side. The nose of the Rammer bounced violently upward and then slammed down again as the rear wheels caught on the lip and Anomalie rose off of her seat. Her upward motion was halted by her head banging against the hatch of the turret and she slumped back down into the seat, her teeth clattering. Disoriented, she tried to regain her bearings by checking the readings in her HUD, but the entire operating system had started a maintenance cycle. She saw a steady stream of code where the sensor readings should be as her entire internal system rebooted. Groggily, her eyes rolling in her head, she leaned to the side of the turret.

Sigil, glancing quickly in her direction, assessed the situation. "Are you ok? Anomalie! Can you hear me?" She moaned slightly and tried to nod. Her blood pressure had dropped and she swooned in the chair as the gyroscopic systems in her ears restarted. "Hold on!" Sigil shouted. "Two klicks will only take a minute or two at this speed. Lean back and keep breathing."

She slid out of the chair and fell the four feet past the ladder into the compartment; Mara looked at her with concern and she feebly returned a reassuring smile. She crawled to the open area behind the seats and lay down, sliding back and forth on the floor as Sigil shifted the controls.

"I'll be ok in a sec," she mumbled. "This happens all the time...I sys-crash with head injuries...skateboarding was the worst..." She saw her sensors restart and, in a rush, she felt her blood pressure normalize. She took in a deep breath and the vertigo went away as her gyros spun up. "I'm ok!" she called out. "Should I shoot something else?" She pulled herself off the compartment floor, using the back of Mara's seat to steady herself.

"No time," replied Sigil. "Most likely, there will be a drone incoming. The patrol will have called it in. We are almost there anyway."

Anomalie made her way up to where Sigil sat, patting Mara on the head as she passed. "Shouldn't I try to shoot it down or something?" she asked. She was aching to get back into the gunner's seat. When she remembered what it felt like to squeeze the triggers, she thought it was perhaps the finest moment in her life.

Sigil shook his head. "The gun won't elevate far enough to follow an airborne target. We have to dump this vehicle. Can you tell me what I'm looking for out here? What do these 'Crax' look like?"

It was Anomalie's turn to shake her head. "I don't know. I just know that they're out here in this direction. Two kilometers. I've never been here."

Sigil seemed to come to a decision. "Alright then. I see some ridges up ahead. They might give us some cover. When we get into them, we get out. Go back and get Mara ready and push anything that seems useful up here by the hatch." She nodded and hurried to the back of the compartment. She slid the ammunition and all three packs to the front, then went back and started grabbing everything that would move. Sigil slowed the vehicle and slid it into a tight turn, the Rammer seemed to go downhill slightly. As the heavy vehicle ground to a halt, he reached down and unfastened his straps.

"Ok, let's do it!" he shouted. "Out. Now." He leaned over to pick up his rifle, slung it, then hoisted his pack to his other shoulder. "Anomalie, pop the hatch, I'll go first." She pushed on the hatch handle and threw the door outward. Sigil hopped out, dropped to a knee and surveyed the surrounding terrain, scanning to the horizon over the sights of his weapon. There was nothing but blasted earth stretching out on all sides, broken by sharp, ridged spines of rock that jutted sporadically between dusty craters. He quickly chose a direction.

"Come on. We're running that way." He gestured with his hand to a ridge of earth that rose sharply above the horizon. "Anomalie, you first. Then me. Go." Anomalie grabbed one ammo can and started running. She looked back once to see if Mara was there and she was surprised to see her sitting atop Sigil's pack as he ran holding two ammo cans. They made it to the ridge and slid into a depression in the ground at the base of the ridge.

They had no sooner found the depression when Anomalie noticed a strange signature in her HUD. She reached out and tugged on Sigil's sleeve. He turned to face her.

"There's something in the air above us." She pointed upwards. His eyes followed her finger and he squinted past the sun as it was setting behind the walls of the Old Zone. "You can't see it. It's too high up there. Judi drone," she finished.

She knew about the drones. You couldn't see them, or hear them. You couldn't fight them or dodge them. They were nowhere and everywhere at once and they could deliver death at any time. Their eyes could see in the infrared and ultraviolet and their ears could recognize a voice in a city crowd. For the first time since Anomalie had met these two strange people, she cursed her poor impulse control. What had she been thinking? You couldn't beat the system, it was too huge and too old and pervasive. She'd been reading too many fanzines and old anarchy journals. She realized that, if she wasn't about to die out here in the dirt near the Crax, she was probably going to be locked up again, only this time for good. She clenched her teeth in disgust and felt a tear well in her eye as she pushed herself to her knees.

As she started to make her way out of the depression, Sigil held her back. She was about to shake his hand off in annoyance when she noticed Mara. The little girl was standing up on the opposite side of Sigil, her tiny hands balled into fists and shaking slightly. Anomalie blinked away the dampness in her eyes and looked more closely. It seemed like there was a slight glow coming from Mara's hands.

Anomalie switched her visual display through different frequencies to get a better look, first UV, then the radio spectrum. Then, she caught it on a microwave frequency. Mara was definitely giving off some sort of heat energy. Anomalie switched to IR and the display went off the chart. Confounded, she sat back on her haunches, watching as the temperature climbed and continued to climb. Mara was now at around 400 degrees. Anomalie was used to getting erratic readings from her gear, but she could feel the heat as it poured off of Mara. Her eyes widened as the temperature went up to 600. Sigil pulled her back and away from Mara; she didn't resist as she was being dragged. She switched off her HUD and stared at the small child, standing alone in the sweltering dust, a white hot corona of energy around her head and hands. Mara was still shaking visibly and she had a furious expression on her face. It looked so out of place to Anomalie, she had never seen Mara look anything but happy and gentle. The white heat seemed to coalesce into a ball, blocking Mara from Anomalie's view. Then, when it seemed like it couldn't be more intense, it shot upward. For an instant, Anomalie thought she saw what looked like lightning in reverse. Energy crackled from Mara into the sky and Anomalie felt a charge run through her entire body, more electrical energy than she had ever experienced. It was as if every cell and circuit inside her was generating a self-sustaining impulse. Then it was over. The heat faded and the white light dispersed like a candle flickering out. Sigil ran to Mara and caught her as she crumpled onto his shoulder. He scooped her up and brought her back to where Anomalie waited in shock.

"What was that?" she exclaimed. "What just happened to her?" Sigil ignored her, choosing instead to focus on Mara's condition. Before Anomalie could ask another question, she heard a faint, high-pitched whine. She looked around, squinting through the blowing dust, but couldn't locate its source. The whine grew in volume and Anomalie thought it had a familiar edge to it. She suddenly realized that it came from above her. She looked up, the whine grew and grew until it became a howling shriek; Anomalie recognized the sound as the scream of a dive-bomber. She had heard it on old footage of news reels from ancient wars. Then, she saw it, hooking out of the fading twilight, an aircraft, burning through the sky like a shooting star. It wailed its way lower and lower until, finally, it slammed into the earth about 200 meters away from where they crouched, raising a huge plume of dirt like an artillery shell. She turned her eyes away as small clumps of dirt and debris landed around them.

She looked at Mara's face and saw a look of exhaustion there. Sigil got Mara's attention and whispered quietly to her until she began to focus on his voice. When Anomalie saw that Mara wasn't hurt, she breathed a sigh of relief and was about to rush to her and embrace her when she was stopped by a sudden voice.

"Oi!" Anomalie's head snapped around and she saw two men walking toward them from beyond the impact crater that the drone had made. "You there…Oi!" She saw through the black, curling smoke that the men were armed and training weapons on them. She switched on her HUD and was surprised to see that all of her systems seemed to be working better than ever. Whatever Mara had done to her hardware certainly hadn't hurt. She felt her nerves fire up and prepared herself.

"Who are you?" she asked warily.

"We saw what you did to the drone," replied the man who had spoken first. "And we think you better fall through the Crax." He lowered his weapon, motioning to his companion to do the same. "If you know what's good for you."

Chapter 4

Through the Crax

<hr>

Of the entrance to the Crax
and of how they were led inside

THEY FOUND themselves walking between the two men in a dimly lit tunnel. The entrance to the tunnel had been well hidden in the midst of the ridges where they had abandoned the Rammer and the destroyed drone. The two men hadn't offered their names but were willing to talk to them as they escorted them through the twisting passages.

"Is this the Crax?" asked Sigil. He was carrying Mara atop his pack as before, but didn't carry the ammunition as he did before. He only held his rifle, cradled in his arms as he walked. The two men had allowed them to stash the ammunition near the tunnel entrance, just as they had allowed him to keep his weapon.

"Not yet," replied the lead man, without turning his head. "The Crax is underneath the Old Zone. And beyond, under the Judicial Grids."

Anomalie couldn't believe what she was hearing. She could vaguely consider that parts of the Crax were beneath the Old Zone. She had barely scratched the surface of her explorations there so she could imagine that there were other sections underground. But under the city? It was impossible. The Old Zone had very limited Judicial patrols, but the city was crawling with Judicials. They were everywhere, in the hospitals, in the schools. Even in the day cares. How could the Crax be right under Judicial noses?

"Are you expecting us to believe that parts of the Crax are actually under the grids?" she blurted out.

The leader never broke stride when he answered her. "Not just parts. The whole city and the whole Zone has holes into the Crax," he said plainly. Anomalie turned and walked backward to see if the rear guard would support the joke but he just looked into her eyes and nodded. She saw that he wasn't smiling. She spun back around.

"But how?" she asked incredulously. "How can they not know?"

"Engineer will show you how. Engineer's better at 'splainin' than I am," continued the leader.

"The engineer?" asked Sigil.

"Not 'The' engineer. Just Engineer. That's his handle. Don't know if he's actually an engineer or not. But he asked for you, and he always has a reason to ask. He'll let you know what you need to know." They could see that there wasn't much more forthcoming from their escort, so they fell silent as they walked on.

After a short time, the tunnel began to dip downward slightly and before long they were actually walking downhill. The tunnel twisted in a serpentine maze and Sigil estimated that they had walked about 5 kilometers. Anomalie could not get a bearing at all; her satellite uplink was useless at this depth, but she still set her system to simply record what she saw so that they could backtrack if they needed to.

Just when Anomalie was getting bored of the silence, the leader halted and turned about. They couldn't see beyond him, the lights didn't seem to illuminate the tunnel as before.

"You go without us from here. We got other work to do." The leader walked past, heading back they way they had come, and the rear guard fell in beside him. Sigil, Mara and Anomalie looked ahead into the dark and Sigil started to walk.

"Wait!" shouted Anomalie. "How far do we go? What's down there?"

"You'll see when you get there. Engineer is waiting for ya." And with that, the two men disappeared down the tunnel they had just traversed. Anomalie trotted forward to catch up with Sigil and Mara, and Sigil put Mara down so that she could walk herself. Her energy had returned, and she appeared to be in better spirits as she scampered along beside them. Anomalie used her holo projection to cast a light ahead of them.

Before long, the passageway widened and they saw two great lights in the distance, far down the tunnel. As they moved closer, they saw that the lights bracketed an enormous, reinforced metal door which completely blocked their path. In the center of the door was a gigantic, formidable looking wheel lock. There was a security scanner set into the wall near the edge of the door and Anomalie felt it when the trio were scanned in. A moment later, the wheel began to turn and they heard massive bolts sliding aside.

The door made a groaning, scraping noise as it swung open and, without waiting to be invited, they walked inside.

What they saw when they entered was a sprawling urban landscape. Nearly abandoned avenues stretched away from them, with street crossings marked by dim swinging lights. The scarred buildings were made of brick and stone and spattered with graffiti; flickering neon signs cast a chilly, electric glow over the few people that wandered on the sidewalks. In the distance, they saw a few cars scattered along the cracked curbs or rolling lazily through the intersections.

Anomalie stood frozen in awe. The scene looked exactly as she had pictured the past, the time before the war. It didn't look anything like the city she had come from, with its sterile, ferro-crete buildings and Troopers on every corner. She watched, fascinated, as a crumpled newspaper page blew and tumbled from one corner to the next.

She felt a tap on her shoulder and nearly jumped, startled. She looked back at Sigil and saw him point toward a young man who was approaching them from the opposite corner. Clad in a creased leather jacket, heavy work pants and combat boots, the man walked toward them with an easy gait. He had a black, woolen watch-cap pulled low to his eyebrows. Midway across the street, he hailed them and called out.

"So, you found the place all right. Come with me, I have a car around the corner. We should get out of here before it gets too late. This ain't really a great neighborhood."

"Who the hell are you?" started Anomalie, but Sigil gently pushed back her impending outburst.

"Where would we be going, if we go with you?" he asked.

The man threw a glare at Anomalie, which she returned in kind, but he answered her question.

"Me, I'm Walter Ego. I live here. Engineer sent me to pick you up and bring you to his place. I heard you dumped a drone up top, and that makes you a friend of mine. I hate drones." He smiled. "Don't worry, hardrock," he said, addressing Anomalie, "we won't jack you. This is the Crax. Anyone who stomps Judies is fine in our book."

Anomalie relaxed slightly and looked to Sigil for a sign. He raised his eyebrows slightly but nodded at Walter.

"Ok, lead the way. Take us to the engineer." He followed Walter as the strange man turned and walked back toward the direction he had come from. Anomalie, with her hand on Mara's shoulder, stepped in behind them.

Walter looked over his shoulder. "Not the engineer. Just Engineer," he said with a grin.

Chapter 5

The Prince

Of Solomon and Thomas Worth
and of the beginning of their search

THE YOUNG man's footsteps echoed as he strode across the courtyard of the Judicial Palace. As he passed the sentries that guarded the interior entrance, they cracked to attention and issued a formal rifle salute. He ignored them and walked inside. Trailing behind him were an assortment of retainers; they nodded at the guards and scurried past in an effort to keep up.

He walked straight past the courtiers and concubines that lazed on the sofas in the receiving foyer and started up the stone stairs that led to the upper rooms, taking them two at a time. By the time he reached the long hallway that led to his father's audience chamber, he had left the retainers far behind. He stood before the double doors to the chamber and hesitated for only a heartbeat before reaching forward and wrenching the doors open.

"They are here, Father. There has been a sign." He stood between the doors, waiting for his father to lift his gaze from the parchments and documents that were strewn across the massive desk, centered on the far side of the room. It seemed as if the older man had not even heard the doors open. His father finished reading the passage that he'd been studying and only then shifted his gaze upward.

Thomas Worth studied his son for a long moment. Solomon was dressed in the formal attire of a Judicial officer. His torso was covered in ceremonial but functional armor made of a synthetic polymer. Formed of matte black and gray plating, it was fitted across his shoulders and chest muscles creating a sleek and lethal image. The armor also covered his upper legs, with hexagonal plate covering the knee. Below the leg armor, he wore the heavy, strapped boots of a cavalry company commander. Under one arm, he held the helmet and integrated respirator system that was the mark of a Judicial Lancer.

The older man finally spoke. "You still insist on going into the field in that ridiculous costume?" He casually laid the parchment aside and leaned forward, putting his palms together and his fingers to his lips. "You do not need the armor and the other officers know it. Probably most of the rank and file as well. Why must you play such a childish role?"

Solomon's face showed only the slightest hint of irritation but it passed quickly. He didn't intend to allow his father to change the subject; he marched across the granite floor of the chamber and, standing directly before the desk, he dropped the helmet in the midst of his father's work. It crashed and rolled, scattering parchments to the floor. His father slowly lowered his hand and arrested its movement. The helmet rocked gently under his finger.

"My sister is here, in this era!" shouted Solomon. "And most likely with that pious mercenary Sitri. There has been a sign from outside the grids. A burst of energy that destroyed a drone. It can only be Mara." He searched his father's face for a clue, a hint of any emotion that might betray his inner thoughts. As always, his father returned his gaze impassively.

Thomas softly rocked the helmet right side up. It settled, its grim mask looking back toward Solomon as if berating him. Thomas' face hardened.

"I asked a question of you," he spat derisively. "When the High Judge speaks to an officer of the Judicial service, proper deference is required. You wear the trappings of a commander, but you forget who commands *you*? This, Solomon, is why you do not belong in the field with dogs. There is too much of the wolf in you." He stood and turned his back toward the door where Solomon's retainers hovered nervously outside. "Close the door, Solomon. I would speak to you privately."

Solomon turned, making a slight motion with his hand. The double doors slammed shut with a loud report, locking the agitated retainers outside. He turned back to where his father stood gazing out of the window behind his desk. Solomon walked around the desk and joined his father in looking out across the city below. Smoke plumed from huge industrial complexes and rose, blocking light from the sun and sky. Through the haze, troop transports and drones lifted off and lowered at various destinations.

"We cannot know if it was your sister, Solomon," began Thomas. "We must wait for proof. There are others that can create such effects, although not naturally. And not alone." He gestured to the city. "There could potentially be someone from this era, from this grid, who could rival your sister in power." Solomon looked sharply in surprise at his father, but said nothing. Thomas continued. "There is a reason that we came to this era. And my question still remains unanswered."

The irritated expression returned to Solomon's face but he remained composed when he replied. "I wear the uniform to maintain solidarity with the men that I fight alongside, father. It is important for them to know that their leaders are also brothers in arms."

His father snorted audibly. "Brothers?" he scoffed. "These dogs? They barely have minds left to recognize their leaders. After what we have done to them, they have been reduced to the apes that sired them. That is the plan, Solomon. To take away the potential in their souls. With no future for them to contemplate or aspire to, they cannot have hope. And without hope, they have only the Gray Mundane. And soon, even that will be entirely blackened." He paused, and put his hand on Solomon's shoulder. "I received the report about the drone early this morning. It fell near one of the entrances to the Crax. They still think that we cannot find all of their hiding places, but they are no safer than rats, scurrying inside our walls." He turned and sat once again, concentrating on his parchments. Without looking up, he waved his hand absently at the helmet before him. "Take one battalion and dig into their holes. Find me the source of that magic."

The Sixth Tale

Under the Grids

Chapter 6

The Hacker

*Of Engineer, his allies
and of the seeds of rebellion*

THE FULL impact of the changes that the Judicials had made to the Earth was just starting to affect him. He was only now beginning to feel the rippled, noisy current as it began to flow across the cityscape. There had been a time when it hadn't moved him so, a time when he still felt the hope that there could be a new wind. Something had given way and had made him jaded and unfeeling, but even without that feeling, in the absence of hope, he was a scientist; he still had a plan.

It started to snow when Engineer stepped into the night shadows and began to make his way through the remains of the city that he had grown up in. He wished that he could find some others that had been through what he had been through but he knew that there was little chance of that. Faced with the thought of a solitary life as a citizen in the grids, he'd sought out anyone, anything that could be a consolation. In the end, he had only found solace in the most peculiar haunts of the crumbling and tattered residue that had been his childhood home.

When he saw where he had ended up, where he was standing, he began to search around for a clue to his status. He knew that there were others near him, he knew that they were watching him for any sign of resistance or hostility. This was their home and their playground and he was an intruder. They knew that he wasn't a serious threat and that he was severely outnumbered, but it was an inborn suspicion and hostility that had kept them alive for all of the years after the war. He saw movement in the shadows and heard soft scratching noises in the gaps of the brick and concrete. He knew that he had arrived in The Crax.

The Crax at night was full and swollen with a weird sort of tension, a discomfort that was not quite pain. The children that moved about through the dark hours often carried with them a light or flame and they were careful to arrange the lights and torches into some sort of decoy, any trick or technique that would serve to draw attention away from the true source of the glow. They had rigged all manner of contrivances to hang the lights from. There were the obvious poles and standards, there were shrouds and veils.

Some of the more clever children had created reflecting arrays from whatever scraps they had managed to scavenge on their nightly rounds. If a child was truly lucky, he may even have acquired a holo generator. The effect was such to cause a gang of roaming children to give off an unearthly glow, a shimmering, translucent shell that would hurt ones eyes if one was to stare directly at it for too long.

The children were always much too frightened to wander alone and with good reason. Without the three-hundred and sixty degree protection provided by the gang, a lone child was sure to go missing. If the gang was attacked or if the children sensed that they were being tracked, the lights could be instantly extinguished. With nary a murmur, the softly glowing orb that surrounded the pack would vanish and the children would scatter, secreting themselves into what available grottoes or crevices could be immediately found. They were quite adept at discovering such places and, in the blink of an eye, a roving band of urchins would seemingly cease to exist.

He watched as the children drifted, wraith-like, through the silent snowfall. They made their way across an open area that was splayed between two large structures just before him. He felt that they knew he was there but had not yet sensed a reason to hide from him. The younger ones kept their eyes fixed upon the leaders, who stayed on the periphery of the group, keeping the smaller ones toward the center. The oldest, no more than thirteen, knew that the presence of fear was often its own cause, a kind of recursion or folding into itself. In his short life, he had learned that to think it was to conjure it and that, many times, to act in courage was to create courage. The boy walked with a swagger across the open, exposed place, scanning to the left and to the right for any enemies or opportunities that might present themselves. He kept himself mostly hidden nonetheless.

Sliding himself into an unobtrusive shadow and studying the children from the edges of his eyes, Engineer pivoted his head to keep pace with the older boy. His mouth was slightly open so that his ear canals would relax, allowing more of his sense of hearing to play over the scene. The Crax was quiet at this time of night except for the occasional chatter of distant gunfire or the muffled rumble of a car sliding through the snowflakes.

The children had that sort of hunger that could be felt in their legs and in the small of their back, a deep hunger that could make you angry at your closest friend and could make it so that you could not think of anything else. Once you had gotten to that point, you were more animal than human, a prowling hunter or scavenger, no better than a rat. You could go beyond even that and become something that made you worse than a rat, you could become a monster. It was a special sort of sin that it could happen to one so young. They began their nightly search for sustenance on the same tired streets that were filled with the more fortunate by day and they conducted their rounds with a feral intensity that belied their tender age.

Engineer waited, motionless, until the gang passed by, then continued deeper into the Crax. He often took varying routes into the underground. Depending on the day, one or another route might be impossible. Each time that he entered the underground metropolis, or 'Fell through the Crax', he entered in a different area. As he moved toward the center of the city, being careful to avoid notice, he took his bearings and adjusted his path. The Crax often changed its appearance and negotiating it took some practice. Although Engineer lived his public life in the Judicial Grids, he had been born in the Crax and his mind rapidly returned to its native habits.

As he made his way to his workshop, he considered what he was about to do. He realized that tonight might be the last night that he was ever inside the city of his youth. His thoughts went back to his own time as a child of the gangs, and how he had been given the gifts of reading and writing. Those gifts had saved him, he realized. And the fruit of those gifts was waiting for him in the workshop now, waiting to be gifted back, waiting to save others. He made his way to the back of a twisting alley, unlocking and pulling aside the gate that was there. Glancing furtively over his shoulder, he went down a small stairway and entered his basement workshop.

Once inside, he moved in haste. He stacked any lab equipment that could be lifted by hand and permanently damaged any larger pieces that couldn't be moved. Then, he stood at an ancient computer terminal and entered the commands that started a deletion sequence. The hard drives whirred and he began stuffing notes into a small blast furnace that squatted in the corner. As the last of the notes burst into flames and he looked around for anything that he had missed, a female holo shimmered into view in the center of the room.

"Meeko-chan," he said, without glancing up at her. "Finally you arrive. I'm already finished here."

"Walter is enroute to this location, yet you seem to be vacating the premises." The holo's words seemed to sound from all directions, but Engineer knew that they were simply resonating in his cochlear implants. He didn't pause in the work of destroying anything that would incriminate or identify him to a Judicial search but the holo continued. "He is with the three that we have been tracking." At that statement, Engineer hesitated. He looked up at Meeko.

She appeared to float in the center of a holographic matrix, yet she was indistinguishable from a flesh and blood person. Her skin tone, hair texture, even vocal quality gave no impression of artificiality. To an outside observer, she would have seemed exactly like any young, pretty and stylishly dressed woman of Asian descent. But Engineer knew better. He had developed the algorithms that allowed Meeko's hair to flow in such a perfect way; he had created the sampling system that so correctly rendered a human voice. And he had programmed Meeko's personality and memory. He felt slightly annoyed to have to explain himself to software that he had built.

"Well then. You will just have to explain to them that it wasn't prudent for me to remain here any longer." He stuffed a few tools into a small satchel and slung it over his shoulder. "Walter at least will be fine. He can simply return to the Label when he's finished."

Meeko nodded but seemed to be unhappy with Engineer's response. Her face became still for a moment and Engineer knew that she was accessing archives on the Label satellite. There was often lag if the weather conditions were not optimal. Her face came back to life. "What about the Archons?" she asked.

Engineer was at the door; he stopped and turned back to the woman who stood in the soft holographic glow.

"They must take them from the Crax. There is no way that I can transport them myself. Meeko, it is imperative that the Judicials do not find those devices! Is that clear?"

She nodded and looked around the workshop. There was no need for her to look, in actuality she was not in the room. Her software was miles above, running on a massive server aboard a satellite. But her gestures and mannerisms were designed to create the impression of realism so she cast her eyes about as if searching for something.

"Walter will not have the ability to move them either. He is strong but this is perhaps too much, even for him." She stared at Engineer, waiting for instructions.

"The three that are with him will take them," he replied. Meeko looked doubtful.

"Are you certain? Do you have an alternative plan of action for me?" she asked with a worried tone.

"There is no alternative," he answered. "If these aren't the ones we've waited for then all is lost. Give them the encryption and the map, then begin the download routine. If the system rejects them, disengage Walter and disappear." He finally allowed a trace of worry to seep into his eyes. "I will be waiting for you at the fallback," he said, and stepped through the door. Behind him, Meeko hovered inside the glow of the hologram and stood very still.

Chapter 7

Allies

THE CAR that Walter led them to was black, red and mean. A 1934 Ford Coupe with a flathead V8, a blower and sidepipes, Anomalie's jaw nearly hit the sidewalk when she saw it. It sat, poised and waiting, like a panther, at the edge of the street.

"An actual hot-rod? Like rockabilly...This thing is s-i-i-ick." Anomalie ran her hand along the door as she got in. Walter grinned at her as he pushed the driver's side seat forward so Mara could climb inside. Sigil, unslinging his rifle, sat in the seat behind Anomalie.

"Yeah, Engineer likes the classics," said Walter. "He rebuilt this thing nearly from scratch. I mean, he actually had to re-fabricate whole chunks of it. But it still looks stock. One of a kind." He started the engine and the Coupe rumbled away from the sidewalk.

Walter tooled through the streets of the Crax, leisurely resting one hand on the wheel, while Anomalie sat in the passenger seat and marveled at the city. Mara peered with wide eyes at the buildings and the streetlights, barely able to see over the door and through the glass.

"Engineer's place isn't far from here," said Walter. "I'm taking a bit of a roundabout, but we'll still get there quick. He should be waiting for us."

As he navigated the car through back alleys and under overpasses, the darkness and snow fell around them and the Crax began to take on an even more ominous mood. Sigil became more alert and Anomalie thought that she saw flutters of movement in her HUD. But, each time that she tried to get a clear reading, the signal would fade away. The Crax looked abandoned but it felt as if there was a pulse of life that trickled through the shadows.

Walter finally pulled the car into a narrow side street and stopped. He turned slightly so that he could address them together. "We're here. This is the place. Now, I'm just giving you a heads up. He can seem a little strange, but Engineer knows his tech. Most of the gear that keeps the Judies off our back comes from him. If he said he needs to meet you, then it's a good thing." He pushed open the door and stepped into the alley, reaching down to help Mara from the car. Sigil and Anomalie got out and followed. Walter led them down a short stairway to a basement entrance and rapped at the door. There was no audible answer but Walter seemed to stiffen; Anomalie recognized the twitch, he was receiving a transmission from somewhere. She tried to track it but her system still showed nothing but silent streets around them. After a moment, Walter's body relaxed and he pushed open the door to the workshop.

They entered the workshop and, amidst the disarray, Meeko stood waiting for them. She was silent until she saw that they were all present and then she spoke.

"Welcome Sigil. Welcome Mara." If Sigil was surprised that Meeko knew his name, he didn't show it. Anomalie registered definite shock.

"You two know her?" She cast her eyes around the workshop suspiciously, annoyance showing in her face. "What is going on? I'm starting to get fed up with being left out here. I mean, how does she know you? How did Mara do that thing with the drone? How—"

Sigil stepped forward abruptly and cut her off. "You are right to be curious. But not right now. I have some questions too." He faced the holographic image squarely. "How do you know who we are and why have we been brought here?"

Meeko's eyes wandered over to Anomalie but only for an instant. She returned her gaze to Sigil and Mara. "You have no memory of when you were awakened? We were activated alongside of you. Walter and I." She gestured to Walter.

Sigil's eyes narrowed as he pieced together what had happened. "Engineer is the person who revived us?" he said. "I find that hard to believe. He would have to be fluent in a number of ancient languages and techniques that are nearly impossible to learn. And I understate the difficulty."

Meeko shrugged and went on. "Engineer summoned you and you came. I do not know that other girl," she finished, throwing a suspicious glance at Anomalie.

"I remember you," said Mara softly. Anomalie shot a hard look at her and shifted uneasily on her heels. She didn't really like the tone that this holo was putting out.

"And I remember you, little one. My name is Meeko. Engineer instructed me to give his devices to you."

Anomalie couldn't keep quiet any longer. "Who is this Engineer? Where is he?" she blurted out. "C'mon Sigil, you have to let me in on what's up here." There was something about the holo that was bugging her, some slight sense of familiarity that Meeko gave off.

"Engineer came and went. He is my creator. And also Walter's," said Meeko.

Anomalie's eyes went wide as it dawned on her. She had grown up around artificial intelligence and robotics, but this was like nothing she had ever experienced. She took a closer look at Walter. He noticed and smiled at her. She saw how his skin pulled taut around his mouth and eyes. It was indistinguishable from any human skin she had ever seen. She looked again at Meeko and saw the same perfect detail. The woman in the hologram appeared as real as Sigil and Mara. Meeko noticed Anomalie's reaction but didn't pause. "There are Judicial troops on their way here. Engineer could not wait, but he left the encryption key here. I am directed to give it to you, Sigil." There she paused. It was as if the pause button was pressed on a vid, her image stood perfectly still as she waited for Sigil's response.

There it is..., thought Anomalie to herself, *uncanny valley all the way...*

Sigil nodded. The mention of Judicial troops motivated him to action. "Very well, what are the devices? Where is the encryption key?"

Meeko's face came back to life. "I can give that information only to you. I am afraid that Engineer's instructions were very clear." She looked pointedly at Anomalie and received an icy stare in return. Sigil seemed to consider this for a moment and then decided.

"Anomalie, take Mara outside and wait in the car. I'll be there when I finish this," he said. Then, he bent closer to her ear and added gently, "I will explain as much as possible as soon as possible. I promise you." Anomalie scowled at Meeko but then nodded and grabbed Mara's hand. They raced up the stairs and into the snowy alley. Anomalie opened the door of the Coupe and lifted Mara into the back seat.

"Buckle up, ok?" she said, making sure that Mara obeyed. When she saw that Mara was in her place, she pushed the seat back and slid into the driver's seat. She put her hands on the steering wheel and waited.

IN THE WORKSHOP, Sigil wasted no time. "I do have memories of being revived in this era. But it is somewhat hazy. I apologize for any offense given." He bowed slightly to both of them.

"None taken, my man," replied Walter. "I won't remember leaving here either. Meeko's gonna deactivate me," he chuckled. "I have *lots* of gaps in my timeline."

"So now, these devices that you mentioned…" Sigil said to Meeko.

"Yes. We must be quick. The encryption key is in a small bundle, hidden below that furnace. Inside the bundle is a device called a fill. An encryption fill. This fill must be inserted into another device to activate the Archons. Like a key into a lock."

Sigil's eyes narrowed, ever so slightly, when he heard the term 'Archons' but he was already at the furnace, maneuvering his hands for a better purchase; the others didn't notice his reaction. The furnace was still warm from the fire that Engineer had burned inside it. Sigil spread his feet and pulled, straining against the weight of the furnace. It didn't budge. He continued to pull. Walter went to the opposite side and bent down. Together, they hoisted the furnace a few inches above the floor and shifted it away from a small compartment cut into the floor. Sigil bent and removed the bundle.

"I have it." He held it out for Meeko to see.

"Very good. Inside the bundle is also a map. You must take the fill to another location. The Archons are there. It is nearby, the map will show you the way." He nodded at her and started for the door but she spoke again. "Please open the bundle and check the map. I was instructed to insure that you understood it." He blew a breath through his nose in impatience but opened the bundle. Underneath a metal encasement with a large connector on one side, he saw the map. He unfolded it and examined it.

"I understand. I see where I'm going." He refolded the map and put it away, inserting it beneath the fill and resealing the bundle.

"Then our task here is done." Meeko's image turned slightly toward Walter. She went still as she transmitted a signal to him and his body appeared to freeze solid. Sigil watched as the last small movements in Walter's fingers stopped and he stood like a statue next to the furnace they had just moved together. Sigil thought that there was something disturbing in the way that the life just drained away from him. Meeko turned back to Sigil. "Please make haste. The enemy is very near." He bent his head to her as he turned toward the door; from the corner of his eye he saw her flicker out.

As THE SNOW DRIFTED softly through the inky black night sky, Anomalie sat and watched her breath curl in great puffs before her face. She thought for a moment that she saw shapes in the vapor, little faces that looked back at her through the veil of mist. She would do the same thing on the hot summer days, sit on the roof of her building and look for structure in the clouds above her. She used to do it when she smoked, in the days before she had quit. There had always been those eyes and mouths in the smoke and the clouds and so she had never really felt alone.

She heard a noise ring across the street to where she sat in the driver's seat of the Coupe. She saw Sigil running between the small bursts of white dusty snow that the wind kicked up as it blew across his path and so she began to roll her window up. "Did you get it?" she asked as he came around the front of the car and opened the door. He didn't pause to look at her or respond until he was safely inside the car and the windows were up and blocking the biting wind. "Where is it?" she pressed. He reached into the folds of his tunic and removed a small package that he had been shielding from the wind and the snow.

"Calm down, I have it..." he said, motioning with his free hand to placate her. Her eyes followed the package as he set it on the car seat between them and, when they were satisfied that it was intact, finally rose to meet his gaze.

"What did they give you?" she asked. She saw that he was tired, and still breathing hard. His fatigue was electric and conducted a bit into her; she felt spent too. She reached down to the keys without taking her eyes off of him and coaxed the car's engine to life. "I don't trust them a bit." she said with a resolute tone. "This sounds like a raw deal if you ask me."

"Just drive," Sigil said, without looking up.

She shifted the car into drive and spun the wheels in the snow. Finally they caught and she slid the car into the street and around in a lazy arc, pointing it away from the building that he had just emerged from.

Sigil was still catching his breath when she spoke. "Now that we have it, whatever it is, what do we do with it?" He glanced over at her and saw something in her face that worried him, a slight manic touch. She gripped the wheel of the car with a sort of rage, as if the swirling eddies of snow had been sent to obstruct her path, visions of an elemental spell that had been cast against her. He slid his hand into the web of the seat belt on the side that faced away from her and furtively wrapped the belt twice around his arm.

"And, more importantly, where are we going with it?" She rounded a corner, taking advantage of the emptiness of the nightime streets and using all four lanes to make the turn. The car fishtailed a few times and once again came under her control, Sigil pretended not to notice.

"We don't have far to travel," he said, as he checked to make sure that Mara was safely secured, "but we must be quick. We are heading to Engineer's fallback laboratory. He's labeled it on this map." Sigil looked up from the map. "Turn right here." Anomalie turned the wheel and the Coupe slid around the corner. "Left after two more streets," he said without looking up. She obeyed and steered the car into a short driveway ramp. She stepped on the brake and, with barely noticeable relief, Sigil loosened his grip on the seat belt.

"Gate's chained and locked," she said. Sigil stepped out of the already open door and trotted rapidly toward the gate. He fished some tools from a small pouch at his waist and began working the lock. Before long, he slid the chain out of the fence and swung the gate open wide. He waved Anomalie in, closing and securing the gate behind them. He returned to the passenger seat, closed the door and looked down at the map again as Anomalie drove slowly through what appeared to be an abandoned warehouse area.

"Around to the rear of that building there." He gestured to the shorter of the buildings and Anomalie followed his hand. They parked the car in the shadow cast by a squat warehouse with darkened windows. "This is it," Sigil said and, a few moments later, they were standing in front of a heavy steel door into the building. He pocketed the map and walked up to the door, but before he could examine it, Anomalie shouldered past him.

"I'll do it. This one's not an antique like the padlock on the gate," she explained as she switched on her HUD.

Sigil hesitated, but stepped back and folded his arms. "A thousand pardons," he said, with a slight bow of his head.

Anomalie knew the lock. It was a common type, manufactured by one of the many security contractors that produced hardware for the Monarchy. It worked by positively identifying the owner by a series of overlapped attributes. It could verify vocal attributes but would only open if they overlapped with retinal attributes. It would also scan other identifying patterns such as facial or DNA attributes. The clever design of the lock relied on not only identifying the owner but, once the owner was identified, it would send a coded key signal to the owner's implants, which would then feed back into the lock microphone, essentially refusing to budge unless the owner was physically standing in front of the door. To make things worse, it would only allow two entry attempts. In theory, it was unpickable. Anomalie snorted derisively, shaking her head.

She began to sort through material that she had downloaded to her system over the years, searching for specs about the lock. Different data about contracted systems had been floating around the grids if you only knew where to look for them and she had learned how to find information in the most accessible places. She'd learned that any large bureaucracy had weak spots, friction between systems that could be exploited simply because the system was so big and cumbersome. Specs had to be copied for maintenance purposes, backdoors had to be developed to make services convenient. People made mistakes, software had bugs and hardware had design flaws. If you were insightful and persistent, anything could be cracked.

She found the manual she was looking for as her HUD ran a script that searched for the particular production series of the actual lock on the door. Simultaneously, she ran another script on the manual. This script looked for semantic connections that existed in the text of the manual. Because the manual had been generated by software, her script could recognize the specific program that had written the document and cross-reference it against a list she kept of known problems that the software had exhibited. Within a minute, both scripts finished. Floating in her vision was a short list of three documented exploits that were effective against the lock. The top one was highlighted in red as the most probable. She paused and read carefully through them. She chewed on her lip as she considered all three, then she puffed her bangs out of her eyes and decided to go with the second one.

She scrolled quickly through her onboard applications and found a sine wave generator and fired it up. "Cover your ears, you two," she muttered. When she saw that they had, she started a series of tones. The first were barely audible but they gradually grew in volume, the last tone sounded shrilly. There was a loud clank as the heavy bolt slid out of the door jamb. She pulled the handle and the door swung open.

"Nice," said Sigil. Mara beamed at her. She tried to look nonchalant as they filed into the warehouse past her, but when they weren't looking, she let out a deep breath, relaxed her shoulders in relief and followed them inside.

Chapter 8

Helix

Of the Archons
and of the power they wield

THE INTERIOR of the warehouse was dark; Anomalie triggered her system and a sphere of light shot out to illuminate their surroundings. It appeared rather barren, with a layer of dust covering various computer terminals and workbenches, full of scattered scraps of circuitry and equipment. They drifted inward and Anomalie ran her finger through the dust on one of the benches, letting out a low whistle. Sigil turned his head to the right and left, searching for a port that might match the connectors on the fill. Mara stood between them and cocked her head curiously.

"What is it that we're looking for?" whispered Anomalie. She picked up a chunk of circuit board with wiring and solder hanging from it. "Pretty gnarly..." she said, under her breath. Behind her, Sigil had found something promising and was unwrapping the bundle that held the fill. "When are you gonna tell me about Mara and these AIs? I figure, now is as good a time as—" Her words held in her throat as Sigil slid the fill into a receiving port below one of the terminal screens. The screen filled with light and a series of symbols began scrolling across it.

Anomalie took Mara's hand and walked near Sigil. She stood by his side, with Mara between them as the glow of the symbols traced light and shadow over their faces.

"I don't recognize this code," she murmured. "It doesn't look like normal syntax..." She tried to make sense of what she was seeing but the symbols seemed to make odd patterns on the screen, emerging from chaotic bursts to form eddies and swirls.

Sigil moved closer to the terminal interface. "I have seen this before." He seemed to be studying it carefully, reading some sort of meaning from the surges of light. He reached out and touched the interface.

Immediately, the other terminals in the workshop came to life and there was a hum from various machines. At the sound, Mara's head twitched and she seemed to be listening intently. Anomalie's head snapped toward the other terminals and she saw that the same pattern was flashing there as well. The visual in her HUD became fuzzy and she heard a high pitched whine in her implants. She winced.

"What is it?" she asked, mentally adjusting the volume in her ears. Mara released her hand and turned her head upward. Anomalie followed her eyes and stared in wonder. Above them, in the floating dust, the symbols cast from the terminals seemed to hang in the air. They formed a kaleidoscopic shape, spinning above them. "Sigil...?" she whispered softly. He didn't seem to hear. "Sigil?" she said again, more loudly this time.

He glanced over his shoulder at the floating pattern and then back at the screen. He touched the interface again and the hum became more present. Anomalie felt it vibrating in her chest and under her feet. The shape above them spun more rapidly.

"Do you hear it?" Mara whispered. "The song?" She was swaying slightly, side to side, her eyes nearly closed with a gentle smile on her face. Anomalie looked at her, puzzled for a moment.

"I only hear that buzzing... I have my volume down..." She adjusted her volume and heard the whine again. Then, she heard it. A soft melody, first in short snatches and barely audible. She made another adjustment and the melody became clear. Her mouth slowly opened in awe. She hardly noticed that Sigil had moved away from the terminal to stand beside them. He touched her shoulder but she didn't turn. A small tear began to form in her eye as she focused on the music that she heard.

It was as if all of the weight and pain of her young life lifted away. Every second of solitude and fear that was in her memory floated to the surface for an instant and then evaporated like fog in bright sunlight. As her mind tried to follow the voices that she heard in the song, they seemed to meld, together with the notes of the melody, into a single passionate lyric. Below it, the sound that she had initially felt as a hum or vibration became a driving rhythm that pushed forward, making her heart race with energy.

Her eyes narrowed, there was a feeling of rage bubbling up inside her but it wasn't a painful anger. She felt freedom just beyond her reach, and the knowledge of it burst forth in a hot eagerness; for the first time in her life, she believed that she could reach it. That was what the voices were saying, and it filled her heart with a glad anger.

Sigil smiled and touched her shoulder again. This time, she felt it and turned to him. He pointed away from them and she saw that what he pointed to was a locked case on a far bench. He went back to the terminal and moved his hand on the interface again. The music faded and the symbols coalesced into code that was familiar to her.

She released her breath in a rush; she hadn't realized that she had been holding it in. Sigil beckoned to her and she blinked, shook her head and swallowed, trying to regain her composure. He walked to the far bench and picked up the case and brought it back to where they stood. He crouched between them and manipulated the lock. Before he opened it, he returned to the terminal.

"Since you could not read the Angelic script, I will let Engineer explain what is about to happen. These are his creations and we should allow him to present them to us." He pressed a key on the keyboard near the terminal and a voice sounded in the warehouse.

"If you are hearing this, I am incapacitated. Unavailable. And this is most likely a worst case scenario in which my main laboratory has been compromised." The voice sounded strong and clear, even through the tinny speakers. Anomalie and Mara both listened, staring at each other while following the words. "My name is Engineer, or that's what I've always been called in the Crax. You are here because we both want the same thing, whether you know it or not. I have made this contingency in order to get the weapons needed to combat the Judicial Monarchy into the correct hands. If you have accessed this message through my encryption protocol, then your hands are the correct ones. Sigil, I'm sure that you realize by now that it was I who intercepted the instructions that you gave to the Order of Dismas, and that it was I who revived you and Mara. I will explain all, but now is not the time. I trust that you have the anchors in your possession. I will allow you some time to prepare."

The voice went silent and Sigil reached forward and opened the case. The two girls looked down and saw what was inside. The case held three small, flat stones. Sigil reached into the case and removed two of them and handed one to each of them. Then, he removed the last one, held it in his hand and stood.

The three of them stood in a triangle, facing each other. Each stone had a hole bored in the center of it, and a chain made of some dull, gray metal was threaded through. Sigil lifted his hand above his head and looped the chain around his neck. He motioned to the others to do the same. As Anomalie put the stone around her neck, she felt a pull from it, as though it was a magnet of some type and was reacting to her implants.

Engineer's voice picked up where it had left off. "Now that you have the anchors in your possession, I will initiate the summoning. I will continue to guide you through the process as it can be somewhat complex. Sigil, you are the only wearer that has handled an anchor before. The other two may reject the wearing. I take no responsibility for your choosing. There must be three and the three must be in harmony. I hope you chose well, Sigil. Let us begin."

The voice stopped and Anomalie saw past Sigil's shoulder that the terminal screen had returned to the strange symbols that she'd seen before. Once again, they were bathed in the light of the symbols and she heard the strange music grow louder. She looked up and saw the shape spinning and it began to form similar symbols on its surface. The light from above joined the shadows below and merged; Sigil reached to his chest and grasped the stone that hung there in his fist.

Engineer's voice erupted from the speakers, but this time it sounded different, clearer somehow. It seemed to be a part of the music as though the song had opened up to make room for a spoken poem. Anomalie couldn't make sense of how that could be, his words were still spoken with the same rhythm, or lack of it, yet they felt in time with the tempo of the music.

Adonaios, Archon of the Sun,
thou art the center and the light.
From the word thou hast been cast into the void.
Unto the word thou shall return.
Forever in motion, well of life and scourge of shadows,
enter into this world of flesh.
Lend us your power.

From the computer system, Anomalie heard a digital transmission but it was far more complex than anything she had ever encountered. Her system was set to track local radio traffic but she felt her processors heat up as they attempted to decrypt the signal. She began to feel faint. The shape that was spinning above them slowed down, and she saw the symbols join together into one bold shape. A brightly shining light burst forth and covered Sigil from head to toe. From inside the chorus of voices that she heard in the music, she heard a single voice become separate. It was a deep and strong voice and it picked up a different melody and began to boldly lead the music. She saw Sigil's mouth moving silently along with the singer and, when the voice seemed to reach a crescendo, she saw the light take shape around him. A low rumble started to affect her belly and she swayed slightly, as though the music was making her drunk. The light solidified around Sigil's arms and chest first, and she saw a breastplate and gauntlets form on him. The solid shapes appeared around his legs next, forming greaves and boots, and finally around his head and face. She began to feel afraid as she saw his eyes disappear behind a helmet.

Slowly, the light faded and she saw Sigil, standing before her, clad in a tightly fitted armored suit. Cast of a burnished golden, metallic substance, it seemed to be made up of different sections for the arms, torso, legs and head but, between the plates were threads of light that connected it over his joints. The mask and helmet were reminiscent of an ancient samurai demon mask, with a slightly feline face. His eyes were covered with a single sheet of material that reflected black. Inside she could see points where his eyes glowed with a red tint. She thought that it looked like the most futuristic thing that she had ever seen, yet frighteningly old all at once. The mouth parted cruelly, almost seeming alive, and she saw vicious fangs at the edges of the opening. Where his rifle had been slung across his back, there was now a long, wickedly sharp spear angling from behind his shoulder.

Engineer's voice spoke again, and Mara's hand rose to clasp her stone.

Horaios, Archon of the Moon,
thou art the silent mover in the night.
From the word thou hast been cast into the void.
Unto the word thou shall return.
Forever in motion, mistress of magic and breaker of tides,
enter into this world of flesh.
Lend us your power.

The digital signal shot through Anomalie's implants and a new symbol formed on the shape and Mara was draped in light. Anomalie heard another voice break away from the chorus and start to sing alone. The song changed and became soft and filled with dark sadness. The voice was gentle and crushingly beautiful and it seemed to sing forlornly of distant loneliness. Mara's lips moved along with it and the light took shape around her. As the light faded, Mara stood armored. Her armor had a cold, silver blue tinge. Above the arm-plates and from the waist there was a gauzy mist that seemed to blow gently in a wind that was not there. It appeared like a translucent skirt over Mara's legs and the sleeves billowed away from the armored plates. Anomalie thought that it looked both lovely and terrifying on the little girl. The helmet fitted tightly to her head with nothing to cover her face. It curved down below her ears and toward her mouth, protecting her cheeks. To Anomalie, it seemed vaguely familiar and then she realized that it was like the armor of a tiny Viking shield maiden. An electric blue Valkyrie.

Engineer's voice rang out once more and again, a different symbol formed above them.

Sabaoth, Archon of Mars,
thou art the blood and the glory of battle.
From the word thou hast been cast into the void.
Unto the word thou shall return.
Forever in motion, bringer of chaos and slayer of men,
enter into this world of flesh.
Lend us your power.

Anomalie felt the tingle of the radio transmission in her ears and she was awash in light. The song began to swell, the underlying rhythm began to pound and come to the fore. Anomalie felt her heart beating and she reached up to her chest and found the stone there. Holding it tightly, she looked upward. Where the shape had been before she could now only see a bright ball of intense light. In the center of the light, she saw a tiny black spot begin to grow. At first, it was just a pinprick and then, like a drop of blood on white snow. Then a crimson, black hole that she couldn't help but stare into. The music was rushing forward in her ears and she heard a howling voice begin to sing alone. It left the chorus a bit too late and rushed to catch up but she could tell from the fevered tone that the singer didn't care. Although she couldn't see the singer's face, she knew that there was a look of rage there. It spat out a staccato refrain and she felt her lips move along with it. The song was one of crucial immediacy, of freedom and protest and angst. But more than that, Anomalie knew it was about violent rage. She saw something moving in the black, and she strained her eyes to see. She saw it was coming closer to her, growing in the dark and that it was a face. She stood her ground, the face came closer and closer until she saw it clearly. It was a helmeted warrior, his teeth tightly clenched, the brows of his eyes furrowed in hatred. She saw him running toward her, a long bloody sword trailing behind him, preparing to swing it forward. She clenched her own teeth, still growling the unknown lyrics under her breath. She felt her stomach muscles tighten as she prepared for a collision.

Suddenly, the vision faded. She let the held breath out of her lungs. She lowered her eyes to see that there was armor covering her body. Made of a dull crimson, the threads between the plates glowed with an angry fire. She felt the helmet around her ears and neck and her vision had changed. There was another system alongside her usual HUD, there were additional icons floating in her eyes just beyond her normal view.

She felt afraid to move but after a moment's hesitation, she held her hand in front of her face and slowly turned it front to back. She could see the new sensor meters scanning data from her hand and its movement but the foreign symbols and digits meant nothing to her. She made an attempt to access the sensors, her mind reaching out through the usual control input of her implants but there was no response. It was as though there was another person's HUD interwoven into her own and the strange sensation of another set of eyes just behind hers, looking out at the same scene.

She was jolted away from her inspection by Engineer's voice; it now sounded apart from the music, as it had before the summoning. "We have summoned three entities into this plane. You now have these entities in harmony with your material body. They have not rejected you; this is good. There will not be time to instruct you fully in the nature of these beings. Only you, Sigil, have a personal history with them. The others that you have chosen must learn about them through trial and error, and this learning will most likely be extremely taxing. I apologize for that but nothing could be done in the short time that I had to prepare this experiment. Sigil, you must guide your friends in using the abilities of the Archons as best they can." Sigil aimed a reassuring look at Anomalie and reached out to Mara to rest his hand on her shoulder.

Engineer continued. "But I will not leave you entirely ignorant. Listen closely! I will tell you what I can. You now wear armor that is the physical form of beings known as Archons. These beings are closely akin to the race that you know as Angelic but, as Sigil can surely tell you, they are as different from angels as lions and tigers are different from house cats. The process that summoned them here was developed by me, in this very laboratory. The technical method that I developed is far too complex to explain now, as is a full explanation of their powers. The stones around your neck are known as 'anchors' and these anchors bind the Archons to the specific DNA of the wearer during the summoning. They can take any physical form, but I chose to design their appearance as armor. There is no particular reason for this. They could appear as animals, or gods and goddesses, or weapons. Think of my choice as a practical aesthetic. You must rely on the Archons and use their power to move against the Judicial Monarchy. Lord Berith, which is the true name of the High Judge of the Monarchy, has begun his final plan." There was a pause and they saw the computer terminals shutting down one by one, leaving only the center one lit. "This is the final part of my message: The Archons with you are Adonaios, Horaios and Sabaoth. You *must* harmonize with them! And you must seek me out so that I may explain in more detail. I will make contact, but until then, fight! And survive. That is all that we can ask of you. One final warning: Berith, and his son Solomon, can easily summon Archons with more ease than I. My method is an imperfect mimicry of theirs. Be vigilant! I will now destroy the traces of this ritual. Farewell, and good hunting."

The computer screen went dark and they were left standing together, the soft glow that the armor gave off was the only illumination.

Anomalie broke the silence. "Did he just say that this armor is alive? I mean, it has a name?" She was still struggling to control her display, there was a flurry of symbols in the corner of her right eye. She blinked it away. She ran her hands down her ribs to her hips, feeling the armor. It felt hot, and the servo assists in her joints surged with energy. She clenched her fists and released, flexing her fingers. "Do you guys have like weird code in your eyes? I do..."

Her words were broken off as a huge explosion rocked the laboratory. The heavy steel door blew inwards in a blinding flash of fire and smoke. Anomalie flinched instinctively as she watched the door whiz through the air, almost too fast for her eyes to follow. It hurtled towards them and, as Mara held up her hands to cover her face, Anomalie pushed forward in an attempt to put herself between it and Mara. She was an instant too late. The door crashed into the tiny child and hit her squarely. It folded around Mara and held fast but did not move her backwards even an inch. Mara pushed her arms outward and the door unfolded and slammed to the floor with a crash.

Through the hole where the door frame had stood, Judicial Legionnaires swarmed into the lab, weapons in their shoulders, firing in short bursts. Anomalie barely felt the rounds impact her as they caromed off of the armor plates. She felt an angry buzz from the armor and an electrical surge shot through her muscles. Her HUD was going haywire and between the chaotic readings she saw Sigil centered in her vision.

Sigil bowed his head slightly and crossed his arms in front of his chest, Anomalie watched as threads of golden light unfurled from his shoulders. They stretched upward and outward, forming a network of interlacing curves.

Then, they became darker and took the form of outstretched wings. Inside the dim glow, there was a hazy image of overlapped feathers but they seemed almost pixelated. The wings opened fully and held still for an instant then, with a violent thrust, they pushed toward the floor and Sigil shot upward in a flash of translucent light, leaving a slight after-image trailing behind him. Anomalie's head snapped upward to follow but she saw only a hole in the ceiling and a cloud of debris falling toward her. Beyond the hole, she could vaguely see a golden shape angling sharply away.

She reached toward Mara, intending to scoop her up and rush toward cover but Mara was too quick. The small, armored figure took a step backward, setting her boots into a sideways stance, her gloved hands rising in front of her. She made a series of rapid gestures, tracing a symbol in the air in front of her. Anomalie recognized it as the same language that had been written on the computer screens during the summoning, the same language that was now vying for space in her HUD. The symbol actually hung visibly in front of Mara; Anomalie could not be sure if it was a digital rendering of energy in the air or if it was somehow written in some eerie, liquid light. Before Anomalie could react, she saw a figure superimposed over Mara's body. It was as if Mara had two shapes, that of a little girl and, beyond it or around it, the figure of a woman. The woman was wrapped in flowing, ice-blue fabric, and as Mara pulled one arm back and pushed her other arm forward, the shimmering shape of a bow formed in the woman's hands. Mara uttered a syllable that Anomalie couldn't understand, and the bow released with a crack like lightning. There was an ozone smell and a bolt of energy flew toward the legionnaires as they were dispersing into the room. The bolt exploded in the center of the enemy, scattering them smoking to the floor and blasting an even larger hole in the wall. Mara leaned her head slightly forward, and shot through the hole and into the parking lot outside.

Anomalie was dumbstruck. For a moment, there was silence. Then, she heard something. A voice spoke. "Go. Fight." At first, she thought it was from the implants near her ears but then she realized it was coming from another place. Both inside her head and from outside of her. She heard it again. "Do not be left behind in battle." The voice was the same one she had heard during the summoning, the voice of the singer that had sung with such rage. Outside, she heard the chatter of machine-guns and the pop of rifles and she felt the same as when the warrior had flown at her, with his sword keening behind him. She felt eager anticipation, an edgy dismay that she was away from the fight. The armor glowed redly and she felt it burn. A growl rose from her throat and became a battle cry; she felt a pulling from where the anchor hung inside the armor, against her heart. She felt her leg muscles spring and, with blinding speed, she followed Mara.

She entered the battle to see the parking lot filled with soldiers. Tracers flashed across the night sky as the snow swirled down around them. She saw a line of armored vehicles, the forward element of a Judicial Lancer battalion, on the far side of the lot, with heavy guns spitting toward the workshop. There were also dismounted troops, Legionnaires and conscripts, either hunkered down behind cover or running to their next position. She didn't see Mara, but as one of the vehicles wheeled backward and around in a curve to adjust its fire, she saw a shining form alight in front of it. Sigil came down hard, his boots smacking into the snow covered earth as he crouched, causing a small eruption of snow around him. The wings folded into his shoulders as he stood to face the vehicle. She was still running, and she changed direction slightly towards where he stood.

As she ran past him, she saw him folding his fingers in front of him and drawing a symbol in the air. He pushed both of his hands forward and a pocket of force grew outward from the space between him and the vehicle. Anomalie sped forward, with a plume of snow kicking up in a trail behind her. At the same moment that she reached her target, the vehicle that Sigil had attacked lifted into the air and came down perhaps 20 meters away. Anomalie leaped, without slowing, shifting in the air to land on one of the vehicles. In her HUD, she saw a sort of cross-hair form, centered on the gun turret. Without thinking, she attacked with the only weapon she had, her fists. But, as she lifted her arm for the blow, she felt the anchor tug around her neck and a similar, stronger tug from her arm. She looked up sharply to see what had caught her and she saw a dark red sword forming in the falling snowflakes above her shoulder. Without breaking momentum, she swung it down and watched as it sheared completely through the turret and partially through the hull of the vehicle, leaving an orange glow where it had touched. She nearly swung the blade into her own feet but, luckily, the inertia of the heavy blade caused her to topple forward and somersault off of the vehicle. She landed with a thud on her back behind the vehicle, throwing a puff of snow into the air. As she lay on her back, momentarily stunned, she saw Sigil track across the sky above her, trailing a star-like haze behind him. Her gyros spun rapidly, compensated for her horizontal position and recalculated. She rolled and spun herself to her feet and swung the sword again, neatly slicing the top half of the vehicle from its wheels and tracks. The engine, screeching convulsively as her blade tore through it, ground to a halt.

The turret in the next vehicle spun wildly, the gunner searching for the origin of the attack. Anomalie turned, looking to both sides across the parking lot, assessing the battlefield. She held the sword loosely, her arm held slightly away from her body, breathing heavily. The cross-hair reformed in her vision, this time centered on the nearest vehicle. She pulled her arm back, and began to trot and then run toward the vehicle. The gunner found her as she approached and leaned on the trigger. The heavy, armor piercing slugs smashed into her chest and legs as she picked up speed but she felt nothing as they ricocheted away. She swung, and the blade cleaved through the vehicle's armor as she followed through the opening she'd made. She shouldered aside the immense hunks of metal and chopped the sword back again. She exploded through the hull of the vehicle on the other side and continued down the line, hacking and cutting through the remaining vehicles.

When she finished, she stopped and turned to see the burning wreckage behind her. She saw chunks of red hot metal, spewing sparks and hissing as the snow fell on the fire. The heat was intense as the fuel from the vehicles caught fire and spread into the parking lot, quickly melting the snow and scorching the concrete below. Through the smoke and flames, she saw an ice-blue glow on the opposite side of the lot, flashes of electric light pulsing from it. She ignored the shouting and screams from the surviving stragglers of the remaining vehicle crews and ran towards Mara.

Mara stood facing the remaining infantry. Most were retreating in confusion, shouting harried orders through their respirators, but a few were trying to cover the retreat, returning fire while leapfrogging back through the sporadic cover offered by abandoned vehicles and storage containers. Mara was systematically launching bolts of energy in their direction, calmly tracing figures in the air, then setting herself in her archer's stance and releasing. The remaining covered positions were obliterated into shards of hot, charged metal. As the last of the grunts withdrew out of the lot, Sigil and Anomalie arrived together. Mara lowered her hands as Anomalie ran to her side and Sigil dropped out of the sky to land near them both. The three figures stood alone in a field of destruction. The building that held the workshop was becoming engulfed in flames and the tattered remnants of an entire Judicial Lancer battalion lay in pieces around them. Sigil put his hand to his chest, uttered a word and his armor faded like the snowflakes that were slowly falling around them onto the burning pavement. Once again he was in faded gray, his rifle held loosely at his side.

"Nice," said Anomalie breathlessly. "How do you turn it off? I mean, how do I turn him off or whatever?"

"Simply hold the anchor and concentrate on solitude, as though you wish to be alone with your thoughts," said Sigil. "The Archon will retreat into its own solitude."

Anomalie did it, reaching toward her chest and wrapping her hand around the anchor. The armor seemed to part as her hand approached and then the anchor was simply laying against the cloth of her jacket below. She held it and thought of being alone. As her mind turned to memories of her favorite places, places in the Old Zone where she would run to escape school, or her father, the armor faded and the sensation of another set of eyes behind her own disappeared. "Wow," she breathed.

She looked toward where both Mara and Sigil were contemplating the battlefield, expressions of sadness on their face. Anomalie looked as well and saw both dead and wounded in the snow, the muffled cries of the dying muted by the soft roar of the flames. She thought of how the Judicials had treated her and the other citizens in her grid and she spat onto the hot concrete at her feet and looked away.

They turned and walked back to the workshop to discover that the Coupe was still intact and only covered by a thin layer of soot from the burning building. Sigil motioned to Anomalie to take the wheel as Mara crawled into the rear. Anomalie started the engine, backed out into the smoky lot and began to drive past the wreckage and bodies of the Judicial soldiers.

"I saw a clear route from the air. Go in that direction," Sigil said, directing Anomalie to the path that the battalion had entered by. She drove through a jagged hole that had been cut in the fence in the rear of the buildings and turned onto an adjacent street.

"Where to, boss?" she asked, checking the rearview mirror to see if there were Judicials following. Sigil pulled the map out of his tunic and, dragging his finger across the creased page, traced a line from the warehouse to their destination.

"A level below this one, even deeper than the Crax. Engineer's map is an old one. I recognize some of the roads and I think I know where we are." He motioned to her to turn and she did.

"What's down there besides old subways and rats?" she wondered aloud.

He looked up from the map and peered through the windshield into the falling snow. "We are going to find a church," he said grimly.

Chapter 9
Outlier

*Of Solomon's report
and of his father's response*

IN THE CHAMBERS of the Judicial Palace, Solomon appeared once again before his father. Furious, he paced to and fro, his thoughts on the recent battle. Thomas Worth waited patiently for his son to speak.

"She was there, father," fumed Solomon. "It was Mara and that upstart Sigil. As I suspected, they are here, in this era." He spun toward where his father sat at his desk. "And there were others. Three Archons were there, summoned somehow. And there was another girl."

Thomas glanced upward at Solomon's words. "A second girl? Young, like your sister?" His brow furrowed with the question.

"No, no. Not like Mara," replied Solomon. "Older, and wilder. Perhaps a teen. She was with the Archon, Sabaoth. He manifested as armor and a sword of flame. Together, they nearly destroyed an entire reinforced battalion." He ground his fist into the palm of his hand, calculating the losses. "The older girl disabled the armor attachment herself. If I had been there, it would have gone differently..."

Thomas Worth stood and walked around to the front of his desk. Reaching out, he interrupted his son's pacing with a firm hand on the youth's shoulder. "Someone has performed the summoning magic. The Archons would not come here of their own accord. Some mage of great power has brought them here. You must not only find your sister but also this summoner."

"Could they not have discovered your plan, and moved to protect Mara?" asked Solomon. "I'm sure the Archons have no love for us. Not after we've bound some of their number."

Thomas shook his head. "No, no... They've never really shown much interest in the concerns of men. They must be bound, and by specific arts. No mortal could have done it. I'm almost certain of it. But..." He paused, a troubled look clouding his face.

"What is it, father?" asked Solomon.

"It is not only the summoning that concerns me. It is this girl that you mentioned. How is it that Sabaoth serves her? Mara and Sigil, their powers can be explained; they are of Angelic stock. But this other girl... She cannot be from this era, from the grids. You must find her as well and bring her here. This question must be answered."

Solomon nodded and was turning to leave his father's presence when he was stopped by a thought. "But what if she *is* from the grids? What if she is from this era? What then?" He turned back to face Thomas.

Thomas had moved to the large window behind his desk that looked out across the Judicial Grids. He stood and contemplated the scene with his hands clasped loosely behind him. He looked at all he had wrought: the vast cityscape of Judicial administrative structures, the incessant comings and goings of police and military vehicles and personnel, the thick, stifling layers of industrial and educational and medical progress and, just beyond all of it, the stacked ferrocrete boxes of the residential grids, stretching out to infinity. After a long moment, without turning away from the window, he replied. "This. The Monarchy. All of this was designed with one goal. For one purpose. To halt the perception of hope in the human soul. To wrest control from nature and funnel information directly into the human psyche. Essentially, to enable us, you and I, to act as middle-man between reality and human consciousness."

Solomon waited impatiently; he had heard the theory before. He had some understanding of the ultimate aims of the Judicial Monarchy. He had been immersed in the history and lore of the Judicial Rising since he had joined his father at the Abbey. Together, they had manipulated time and space and, with the assistance of the Archons that they had bound, they had built a great, new order on Earth. In the temporal experience of the citizens, it had taken nearly two-hundred years; in Solomon's perceived passage of time, it had only taken ten. But, he had still heard this lecture many times in those ten years. He began to turn away.

"Hold, Solomon," uttered Thomas, "I've not finished." Solomon stopped, halfway facing the door. "If this girl is from this era, then there is a chink in our armor. Something that we've missed or overlooked. It must be found. Do you understand?"

Solomon understood the how, but he had never understood the *why* of his father's obsession with returning to his rank and position. In a low voice, without turning back to face him, he asked the same question he had asked a hundred times. "Father, why must you go back. Why serve the masters who exiled you for the same crime that they had committed?"

Thomas lowered his head and answered. "Why? Because, I feel this queasy hunger that sits laughing in my belly; it burdens me like a stone and weighs on my center. I want to push it from me but it haunts my guts and makes my hands shake when I sit and think. I wrack my mind to recall just exactly when it began, desperately in search of some small hint of a cure but I cannot remember clearly. It seems now as if it has always been with me, hiding inside my core but if it had, I'm certain I would have murdered myself to rid me of it. I feared that I would never had made it past my exile with such a dread lurking within me. Yet here it is now, like some ancient rival that I had forgotten but whose voice rekindles the same old hatred, the same old scowl. Oh, I hate this, this Onlyness. I hate this feeling of being stalked by God and his company of Angels. To what purpose was this exile and war? To what purpose, this solitude amongst the stars. Why would he send us here to fight an unwinnable campaign?"

Solomon realized that his father had forgotten that he was there. Once again, he was deep inside of his dark memories and bitter anger and he'd replied with an answer that explained nothing. Solomon scowled, and walked to the door. Behind him, his father was still speaking, only to himself, wringing his hands near the small of his back. Solomon pulled open the door, stepped out and closed it behind him. He could not listen any longer. He had his own dark memories and bitter anger to concern him.

Chapter 10

The Message

Of the Fate of Father Dante
and of The Order's Last Stand

ANOMALIE followed Sigil's orders as he guided her through the darkness of the Crax. They took streets where the buildings were gutted even more deeply and the asphalt of the streets was in ruins. Eventually, the Coupe could go no further and they pulled it into an opening that they spied on the edge of a crumbled block and prepared to continue on foot.

They pulled their backpacks from the rear of the car and stood, studying their surroundings. Sigil held the map in front of him and compared it to the layout of the landscape.

"This way, I think," he said and stepped off, guiding Mara with one hand. Anomalie walked behind them, periodically walking backward in order to check the rear.

"It looks like we're alone out here," she said softly. Sigil grunted in reply. "How are we supposed to get further underground?" she asked.

"The map shows an old subway entrance near here. There are markings that describe a tunnel to the church," he said. He shifted his path to the left and they stepped off the sidewalk and began to make their way through a decrepit playground. "It should be just on the other side of this park."

Their boots kicked through the softly drifting snow as Anomalie studied the buildings that lined the edges of the open playground. Cast in dark shadow, the buildings seemed to lean inward above the park, crowding around like bullies over a frightened victim. Inside the park, there were fallen swing-sets and a single, leaning basketball hoop, lonely at the edge of a cracked court. It all looked like something from an archaic myth to her. They reached the far side of the park and found the entrance to the subway.

They quickly made their way to the bottom of the stairway and hopped over the turnstile, lifting Mara over the barrier. At the edge of the platform, Sigil checked the map again, and lowered himself to jump onto the tracks. He held his hands up to Mara and carried her down with him. Anomalie hopped down to join them and they started down the tunnel. About a hundred meters into the tunnel, Sigil stopped in front of an alcove that was set back away from the tunnel wall. He studied it for a moment before stepping inside and running his hands along the edges of the grimy back wall. When he found what he was looking for, he pressed his hands into it, pushing open a small opening at the rear of the alcove. There was a narrow ladder well that descended into the darkness below. He stepped onto the ladder, motioning to Anomalie to help Mara to take her place above him. When they had gone down a few feet, Anomalie followed. She projected a light so that they could see where and what they were descending into.

When they reached the bottom, Anomalie expanded her light, revealing that they were in an open area with a much larger width than the subway tunnel above. There was a passageway that opened to one side and they entered it. At the start of the passageway, the walls and floor were plain and barren but as they continued on, the passageway took on greater embellishments and decoration. Soon, the passageway turned into an ornate hallway with arches spread across the ceiling and with carved statues below.

As they walked, Anomalie felt the mood become somber and silent. Although they had not said anything to each other for some time, she felt as if, now, she should remain quiet for some unknown reason. She noticed the change in both Mara and Sigil as well. Her companions seemed observant somehow, as if they were thinking hard.

Before long, the hallway ended in a wall carved with writing. Anomalie recognized the writing as the same language that she had seen during the summoning of their armor. In the center of the wall, there was a plain and unadorned wooden door with a large ring for a handle. They paused before the door for a moment, and both Sigil and Mara made a strange sign with their hands above their hearts. When they finished, Sigil reached forward, grasped the ring and pulled the door open with a loud creak.

They walked forward into a room such as Anomalie had never seen. Her eyes widened as she attempted to take it in, but it was as if she could not rationally comprehend the space set before her. The walls climbed upward to a high arched ceiling, where painted figures of angels and other beings were locked in battle, their hands holding ancient weapons and their eyes glaring wildly. Below the painted ceiling, the walls were sectioned and each section contained a tall, intricately detailed, stained glass window with soft multicolored hues radiating inward. The windows were decorated with more scenes of combat and even stranger events that Anomalie could not fathom. Each section of wall had immense statues placed between them, the carved figures depicting fierce winged beings that appeared only partially human. The room contained huge, granite columns, at least twenty feet in diameter, which held the roof aloft. Each column was inscribed completely with the strange language that had summoned the Archons, spiraling in drifting patterns up and around them. The room stretched forward, toward a raised altar arranged at the far wall which had a multitude of glowing candles placed above it. The floor was laid with a pattern of interlocked stones that formed a complex geometry, splaying outward from a central point. The overall effect was astonishing and yet serenely still.

Quietly, softly closing the door behind them, the three figures walked inward, the vast space dwarfing them inside it. They approached the center of the room and when they were standing above the central shape on the floor, both Mara and Sigil dropped gently to one knee and made the same odd sign that they had made before they had entered.

"What is that? That sign?" Anomalie whispered timidly. "What does it mean?"

"It is a simple ritual, a token of recognition," Sigil said when they had finished and were again standing.

"Recognition of what?" she prodded.

"Recognition of certain principles and laws. Divine principles, divine laws," he said. He motioned to her to follow and they moved through the center of the room, approaching the altar at the far edge.

Anomalie was still aghast at the size of the room, her eyes playing across the windows and statues as they walked.

"How is this happening? I mean, this building. It's too…big to be here. We didn't come down this far. That ceiling can't be that high…" she hesitated. "I mean, can it?" she added, uncertainly.

"The rules of physics, as you've come to understand them, do not apply fully in this cathedral. I am also starting to suspect that they have been altered throughout the Crax as well."

"I figured that out already." She flipped her finger against the stone hanging from her neck. "These Archons or whatever aren't normal hardware according to any tech specs I've ever seen. So they run on different physics? Different rules?" She could imagine that there were subtle misassumptions in the current, accepted understanding of physics. She'd studied hard, and knew that engineers were always pushing the envelope. "I can grok that."

Sigil shook his head. "Not merely different. Divine. As I said before, divine principles and divine laws."

Anomalie had never been inside a church before. Sure, there were cults inside the grids; people were always buying into some weird belief system. You could believe in people who would sell you hot products, you could believe in philosophies that would make you look hot and feel special, you could even live forever, your consciousness uploaded into some database somewhere. She'd read about it. But to her, it was all just hype and she could never afford it anyway. But as she looked upward at the walls of the cathedral, she knew that this wasn't the same thing. This building, her two companions and the armor that she had worn, weren't just hype. So she pressed.

"So, these divine laws are different than regular physical laws. Okay. Got that. And that has something to do with how the Archons work, and how Mara shot a drone out of the sky, and why she's so important?" she asked imploringly. "Help me out here, Sigil. I'm not a great student, I barely go to school as it is."

"I can explain some, but not all to you. Not because I do not wish to, but because I am no teacher. I cannot explain it as clearly as others can. Here, in this church, we may be able to find clues left by better teachers than I. And, I hope, we can find our next course of action."

They reached the altar and stood before it. Sigil stepped up and, motioning to Anomalie and Mara not to follow, he began to examine the area at the back of the altar.

"How do you know what you're looking for?" Anomalie called out, "Is it on Engineer's map?" She glanced nervously back at the door they had entered by, listening for signs of other intruders.

"No. I know this place. This church is not really in the Crax. Or even below it in reality. This church is something like a pivot. A place that never changes, when all around it changes. Do you understand?"

Anomalie paused and then nodded. "Sure. Like the hinge on a door right? The door moves, the hinge doesn't. A pivot. I get it." She put the tips of the fingers of both hands together and made a pivoting motion.

Sigil stopped searching and pointed at her. "Affirmative! When other things change throughout time, or even space, this church continues. These buildings were built on specific points in the grids. They were the initial landing areas for the angelic race. Places where we fell." He continued his search.

Anomalie stared at him in shock. *"We* fell?" She looked down at Mara, and then turned her head back to Sigil. "Do you mean to tell me that you two are angels? Real angels? Like with harps and wings and halos?" She began to laugh and then she paused, remembering the sight of Sigil flying upward through the roof of Engineer's laboratory. She also thought of the voice recording that Engineer had left for them. She hadn't understood most of it, but she had wondered at the references to angels. Until now, she had been operating under the assumption that the armor and Mara's attack on the drone had something to do with classified Judicial tech. The Monarchy was always developing strange technology and often tested it on the inhabitants of the grids. Anomalie had guessed that Sigil was some sort of military contractor or espionage agent. He had the military look and attitude, it just made sense.

She also didn't really know much about angels. She had seen images in vids and graphics, she knew that they were supposed to do good. People had expressions for it. *You have a guardian angel, kissed by an angel* and so on. But after seeing the way Sigil and Mara had taken apart that Judicial ordnance, Anomalie was certain that nobody would want to be kissed like that.

"Not Mara," replied Sigil. "Only me. And I was kicked out. We go by another name after we fall." He couldn't seem to find whatever it was that he was searching for. He stood up with a rather frustrated expression. Stepping back off of the altar, he began to rummage through Mara's backpack, passing Brownie to her to hold.

"Are you serious?" exclaimed Anomalie incredulously. "Then what is Mara? Is she even human?" Mara looked at her with raised eyebrows when she heard her name mentioned. "No offense, hon." said Anomalie with an apologetic tone, waving her fingers at Mara. "It's okay if you're not. Most of the humans that I know aren't much in the way of awesome, so don't be ashamed. I'm not a bigot or anything." She returned to questioning Sigil, "Is she an alien or something? Or a mutant? They had mutants back in your time, right? With powers? I saw some vids about that once…" She was beginning to chatter excitedly because Sigil was talking openly to her. Hopefully, he would finally offer some kind of explanation.

"Hold on," he said, in an slightly exasperated tone. "Just hold on. If I can find some type of information from around here, I will be able to take us to a safer place and—"

Another voice echoed from the shadow of one of the columns, "There is no safer place than this one, Sigil." All three of their faces turned as one toward the voice. Anomalie lowered into a fighting stance, and Mara's hand reached toward the anchor around her neck. From behind the column, a hooded figure emerged. As he stepped into the light of the candles, he lowered his rough, woolen hood and bared his face. "Hello little Mara." he said, a gentle smile on his face. "I've waited a long time to finally meet you." With his right hand, he made the same strange sign above his heart that Sigil and Mara had made earlier.

When Mara saw the monk's robe and the sign, she released the anchor and rushed forward. The monk held his arms wide and bent at his waist to greet her. She leaped into his arms and embraced him.

Sigil saw the confused look on Anomalie's face and stepped forward to explain. "Anomalie, this is a friend. He is a priest from our order." The monk walked closer, holding Mara's hand in his own and nodding in confirmation.

"Yes, yes… this is so. I have been tending the altar here each day for many years, waiting for you. At last, you have come! And now, the new wind can blow. The tide can finally change." He held his hand out to Sigil and it was clasped in a strong greeting. Sigil pulled the monk toward him and they embraced like old comrades. They stepped apart and Sigil's eyes smiled.

Anomalie hung back with an awkward expression on her face but Sigil put his hand on her shoulder and pulled her forward.

"This is Anomalie Harper. She is with us now," he said.

"And she too wears an anchor I see! Strange times, strange times these have truly become. She is from this era?" asked the monk. He shook Anomalie's hand and bowed his head to her. Anomalie started to relax a bit and smiled at him slightly.

"Hello..." she said. "Yep. Grid four-six-four-niner. Born and raised," she quipped.

"Very good, very good," said the monk. "I am Brother Demen. An acolyte of the Order of Dismas. Sigil has revealed our order to you?" Anomalie shook her head, looking sideways at Sigil with a shrug.

"We have been greatly pressed for time..." began Sigil, but Brother Demen bobbed his head, understanding.

"Yes, yes. Of course. Of course. Well then, I will explain. Come, come, come. This way." Ushering Mara before him, he led the way to the side of the altar. "I am the sacristan of this cathedral." He looked at Anomalie and saw that she didn't understand. "I tend the sacristy. This way." At the side of the altar, he held his hand near the wall, tracing his finger lightly along the granite block. A bloom of script emerged from the stone and followed his finger. He wrote quickly and, with a flourish, finished the calligraphy. A portion of the wall seemed to go out of focus and blur. He waved them through, Mara first and then Sigil and Anomalie. The monk followed them through the opening.

"This is my sacristy," Brother Demen said and waved his hand over the room. Anomalie looked back to where they had entered and saw that there was only an unblemished stone wall. She remembered Sigil performing the same trick, when he'd revived Mara below the Bunkers. She turned back to the place they had entered. The room was dark, with only a few candles set into small alcoves in the walls, but the old priest quickly lit more. He also started a fire in a cast iron brazier set in the corner of the room. Sigil seemed to relax, unslinging his rifle and leaning it against a wall in a corner. Brother Demen found food and drink for them in one of the many cabinets and soon they were seated in a comfortable circle around a low table.

Brother Demen began to speak in low tones. "Before we discuss any other matter, I must relay a message from Father Dante. I've memorized it, as did the brothers who held this post before me. In this way, we tried to insure that the message would only be given to you." He paused and looked at Sigil directly, then went on. "I must admit that my faith was strained. For many years, I was certain that your coming was merely a myth, perhaps something to test us in solitude. But, when I saw the three of you enter the nave, I immediately saw you for what you were. I knew in my heart. Please, accept my gratitude for coming."

"I understand brother, and there is no need for thanks. But, please, the message..." prompted Sigil.

"Oh yes, of course...of course. The message. It begins thusly..." Brother Demen folded his hands piously above the table, lifted his eyes upward and began to speak in a sonorous tone.

"How could it be that those who were once so close could drift away like clouds? How could they be so transient; or was it you who was the drifter and rotated away, a heavy mass, the spinning Earth beneath them? Did they remember the solid reflecting surface, the pull of the waves beneath them; did they ponder the depth

of the sea that was your vision? We think they did not. We think they were as wispy and thin as those same clouds. There was nothing to them, no substance, no form. They were filmy and draped atop each other like cheap garments, yet they hid themselves from each other and from their own sight. They looked anywhere but where there was gravity because they abhorred what was grave and sought to levitate away.

"The Angel's Blood or the Demon's Stone, which will be the marker on our path? Will the path lead to the right hand or to the left? The blood is not the blaze on the trail, the stone is not the cairn. It is the SONG that will guide us to your holy voice, to our appointed reward.

"The Abbey is lost, the brothers scattered, but have we died in vain? The child is thrown into the sea of time. This message is for her and for her protectors, the wearers of the stone and the bearers of the blood. They must seek the Litany of Stars and begin the chorus anew. They must sing the verses as they are written in the book. Only the singer can finish the task that we've begun.

"We must find a new way, a better way, a deeper way. When will we be released, O Lord? When will the new wind blow? How many more days and how many more nights will you keep us in bondage to this system? When will you come to our rescue and show us the extent of your love and kindness? We will not fall into the morass of this world and become bound with the wicked. We are filled with the temptations of the flesh and each day becomes a battle that we are compelled to wage. We walk the path and stumble but you are there to pick us up. We stagger and shake but you are there to guide our stride. This world is made of confusion* *and consternation. We live with our eyes shut. We must see past the misery and death of the heart, We must find our way.*

"O Lord, when we move through the vastness of void, we see that all around us is light. When we move through the depths of the sea, we feel thy warmth. You are always there beside us, you are all that there is and can ever be. All dimensions are your realm and all times are your time. We cannot see past or through you. All that we have ever known is you and the absence of focus on you is why we feel alone. This solitude is the cause of all of it. This separation from you is why we struggle. Please make us whole again and join with us in knowledge. Show us thy love and thy light so we will no longer have to hate and steal and kill. Amen."

When he was finished, he unfolded his hands and bowed his head. Sigil sat quietly pondering his words and Anomalie rushed to comfort Mara as she burst into sudden tears.

The Seventh Tale

Revelation, Hope and Strife

Chapter 11

Dogma

Litany

Bearing many names,
Wearing many veils,
Alone above the piercing lights
The Speaker weaves his tales.

First among the stars,
Last upon the field,
Alone below the cracking earth
The Fallen now are sealed.

The heroes and the scorned,
The regal and despised,
Both bear the mark of time and toil
And end their days disguised.

The Seventh Tale

When will the promise be
fulfilled and justice done?
Only when the Fallen claim
their places in the sun.

A riddle was first posed,
With ne'er a hint or key
The chorus saw the prize held high
above their bended knee.

With faith and trusting souls
The vast and burning lights
Moved across the distant dark
to claim their offered rights.

A host was raised in haste
To halt the drifting spheres
And in the reaches of the dark
The host was met with spears.

The shining blades were poised
But none would strike a blow
Would the faithful be cast out?
The chorus did not know.

The host bore down upon the lights
And the planets as they turned
The shining blades were driven home
As all the heavens burned.

With torn limb and shattered helm,
A clash of sword and fire
The Speaker spoke the words of war
And proved himself a liar.

Dogma

The chorus fled in disarray
Across the sea of time
And in pursuit, the messengers,
In judgment of their crime.

Harried, broken, at long last
They gained a hideaway.
Yet in the harbor that they found
Another judgment lay.

The chorus, and the host as well
All began the same.
Both were born of light and song
But some would end in shame.

Some were given jewels,
And some were given thrones,
And only those with loves on Earth
Were cursed and given stones.

BROTHER DEMEN offered to tell them what he knew of the Abbey's history. "The Order of Dismas was nearly destroyed when the Abbey fell. Dante and the others fought with as much strength as they could muster, but the Judicials were far too powerful. Without Mara's power and your skill, they were lost," said Brother Demen.

Sigil nodded gravely. There was no need for him to explain what he and Mara had gone through at the Abbey, the monk had surely been taught the tale. But, it was much more than a legend to little Mara, her sobs cut into his heart as Anomalie held her and tried to console her. She had lost all the family that remained to her when her father had attacked the Abbey but she had hoped, as he had, that at least Father Dante had escaped. For her, the attack had happened only days ago, and she still was unused to moving through time. The loss of Father Dante and the others had caused a raw wound that would take time to heal. This was also the first time that she'd been without her brother and Sigil was unsure how that was affecting her; Mara still remained a deep mystery to him.

"There were only a few who survived," explained the monk. "Dante made sure to give them the message and instructions to pass it along until you would return. We had no idea when you would return, we only knew that you would be in time. We prayed that you would be in time. And now our prayers have been answered."

"But what does the message mean?" asked Anomalie, over Mara's soft weeping. "Where was this Abbey?"

"In this very place," answered Brother Demen. "This cathedral is the new structure that replaced it."

"The Judicials just let you build a huge cathedral underground?" she asked.

Brother Demen looked thoughtful as he formulated a way to explain. He glanced at Sigil but only received an empty look. Sigil was content to let the priest speak.

"Not exactly…" he began. "This place, this location in the grids is very special. It is here that the exiled Angelic host made landfall on Earth. This was their first point of contact with solid matter. When they fell, there were certain physical effects. Effects on the actual ground. One way to describe it is to say that this is consecrated ground. A holy place."

The priest noted to see if she understood and then continued. "You see, there was a war in heaven. The angels had split into two factions. One side wanted a rebellion, and the other wanted to support the creator. The rebellion failed, and the losing side was cast deep into space and cursed to exist in a material form. This is where they fell." Anomalie nodded slowly.

"For us in the Order, much of this is theoretical. We have only learned this history from some writings and other evidence that we have unearthed over many years. We also have the testimony of those that took part in the rebellion and have made contact with us." He paused and looked knowingly at Sigil.

"Nice!" exclaimed Anomalie, staring at Sigil. "You were a rebel? Stickin' it to the man, huh? Cool." Then, she thought of something. "If this was where they first contacted solid matter, what were they made of before that?" she asked.

"They were as beings of light, pure energy. Or so I am told," answered Brother Demen. Anomalie considered this.

"This place creates a sort of neutral zone," continued the monk. "A safe area or sanctuary. The actual appearance seems to shift and morph for different individuals. To some, it might appear as a small chapel in a wooded glade, to others it will be an immense cathedral such as it is now. Sometimes it is a mosque or ashram or temple. It will always be a place of worship. It will take on the character of the surrounding terrain and populace and will be colored by the psyche of those who enter it. So, for you, Mara and Sigil, it is an underground cathedral. Think of it as a church for your state of mind. For Mara and her brother, it was an abbey that served as their school and home for some time."

Anomalie looked down at Mara, comprehending. "So this is where you come from, huh? I'm sorry about what happened here." She brushed her hand through Mara's hair and tried to wipe some of her tears away. Mara buried her face in her chest and hugged her. "So these two are war refugees? Something like that?"

"There is more to it than that. Our scholars have surmised the true reason for the Fall. We believe that the rebellion was allowed to occur."

"It was a setup?" she asked.

"Something like that. Of course, this is only our theory. But it appears very likely. And Sigil has confirmed that he believes it as well."

Anomalie looked at Sigil and he nodded. Brother Demen went on.

"We think that we know the creator's purpose—"

"Yea, you and a thousand other prophets," Anomalie interjected.

Brother Demen pointedly ignored her and continued, "After the Fall, the angels committed a great sin. They began to visit the precursors of our human race. And they began to use illusion to ensnare their minds. These creatures were simple, with the most basic of intellect. But, they had the ability to fully work with matter. This ability, the angels envied. And finally, they began to breed together. And produce offspring, a hybrid of angel and simian. This was the beginning of human consciousness and culture." The monk shifted his weight, the chair that he was sitting in creaked and groaned.

"Our order suspects that the real reason that God allowed the Angelic race to fall and inhabit the simian hosts was to allow this cross breeding. This was to insure that there would be a perfect space-faring race. The simian consciousness was not equipped for faster than light travel because of its linear perception of time and limited spatial perception. The Angelic race could not yet fully interact with matter. The Fall was allowed to cause a merging of races so that the final offspring would be able to traverse all known boundaries in space exploration. The word angel means 'messenger'. The angels brought the message to us. We are the new breed of messenger to even more exotic beings."

"So that means that we are half angel and half monkey? Humans, I mean." Anomalie wasn't sure that she liked that idea.

"Only some humans," said Brother Demen, "and only certain bloodlines. The greatest percentage of human beings developed from a pure primate origin. In truth, after so many generations of evolution, it can be very difficult to discern who among us possesses the angelic trait. After all, the angelic difference is not one of physical change but one of spiritual energy. We think that the hybrids may be those of us who have a greater connection to the holy or sacred. The religiously inclined so to speak."

"You mean people like you, right? Priests and hippies and cultists and whatever. I understand." Anomalie was used to other people saying that they were part of some special group that she could never belong to. Better grades, better neighborhood, better everything. Even better souls.

Brother Demen looked uncomfortable. "It appears to be a reasonable deduction," he said. "But, ultimately, we are not certain of any of this. We grope blindly, with our limited faculties."

The monk then shifted his attention to Sigil and his voice changed in tone; an urgency came over him. "Brother Sigil," he began earnestly, "I have been having strange visions when I am in prayer. I seem to be intuiting a great evil. There is a sense of wickedness that seeps through my thoughts. Can you give me a reason for why this is so?"

"It could be many things, brother. What are the visions?" replied Sigil.

"I have seen faces, beautiful faces. Beautiful and yet terrible and cruel. They are neither angel nor faerie. Those, I have seen before. These are something that none in the order can comprehend. Others have seen them as well," said the monk.

Sigil's jaw was set firmly when he answered. "Perhaps these are things that are not for you to know..." he started, but Brother Demen spoke quickly.

"How did you come by the anchors, Sigil? How is it that a girl from this era is a wearer? Where did you go before you came here?" The monk's voice took on a frightened air, there was a hint of panic rising in it.

"The stones are not what you or the Order think they are, Demen. They are not part of your teachings. You cannot understand them." Sigil tried to placate the priest, but he reached out and held tightly to Sigil's sleeve.

"From where did they come?" he asked urgently.

"From some guy named Engineer," piped Anomalie. "We went there first, but he wasn't there. That's how we..." Sigil looked at her sharply and she knew she'd said too much.

The monk's eyes widened in horror. "Those stones came from Engineer? That heretic?" He yanked his hand away from Sigil as if he'd been burned.

Sigil sighed and came to a decision. "Brother Demen, I'm afraid that Dante was not the only one who left a message for you." The monk looked at Sigil with a puzzled expression on his face. Sigil went on. "When Mara and I escaped the Abbey, we entered into the deep tunnels beneath the vaults. Even the brothers of the Abbey did not know about these passages."

"But the legend tells us that you vanished when the Abbey fell and would return one day to assist us..." started the monk.

"Yes, but *I* left a message as well. The message was left aboard a satellite, encrypted and written in old Angelic. To be discovered by the Order. The message detailed the time and place where Mara and I were to be revived and the method which would transmigrate our bodies into a temporal merge. This is a deep technology, akin to black magic. Lesser ranking members of the Order do not even know that it exists." He held for a moment, considering how the monk might react. "I believe that Engineer cracked that encryption and has control of the satellite. He is the one who revived us," he finished.

"That man is dangerous, Sigil!" erupted Brother Demen. "He has been deciphering Angelic script. He has been tinkering with other, even more dangerous forces. Some of the other brothers think he may have learned how to perform a summoning. I don't believe that is possible, he is untrained and unschooled, but he could still cause great harm. You should rid yourself of those stones."

"Ahhh, brother..." said Sigil, leaning back into his chair. "Come now. You of all people know that an anchor can not be gotten rid of that easily. I would not be here now if one could simply be dropped into the trash."

"You have not used the stones yet, I'm sure? Dear lord, I pray that you haven't. Heaven only knows what that Engineer person could have done to them." Anomalie knew when it was prudent to lie; she kept quiet and watched Sigil for signals.

"Please, brother, do not worry about the anchors. They are our concern. But tell us what you know of Engineer. We must find him, and speak to him. We may need his help," said Sigil.

Brother Demen looked ill, but he nodded. "Sigil, you have helped our order greatly in many conflicts, over many years. I will do whatever I can to assist you. But please, I beg you. Remove those stones from my church. Whatever powers they possess cannot come from righteousness if Engineer was their source." He swallowed and went on. "I cannot say that I know much about Engineer personally, but there is another acolyte who does. He does not condone that man's actions, no! But this brother was born in the Crax, just as Engineer was, and they were once friends. He may be able to help you."

Sigil nodded reassuringly, "Of course, brother, we will leave with the stones. We apologize for disturbing the peace of your church. And we thank you for the help that you have already given to us."

The priest seemed a bit relieved that the anchors would soon be gone. "Yes, yes, I will send a message to the acolyte, and if he can help you, he will. But, you have made some dangerous choices Sigil. You may have put our cause in great peril. Must you always switch sides so easily?" he asked.

"It is in my nature, brother. Things are not always so black and white to me. If they were, perhaps I would have been a monk instead of what I am," he replied.

"Yes, your path has always been filled with conflict and strife. Or so your legend tells us. It seems that your path will continue the same," said the priest disapprovingly.

"But we only have to find this song then?" interjected Anomalie. "And you said that you knew someone who could bring us to Engineer. He said that he would explain more to us," said Anomalie. "Isn't that what the message tells us?"

Brother Demen shook his head sadly. "I wish that I could reassure you child, and guide you along a safer path, but the vision of my mind's eye is unclear, clouded. Will you still seek the Litany? To find it may be all the worse for you and your friends. The Monarchy covets the power of the Litany and of the anchors. They too must seek them before they begin their journey home."

Sigil shook his head. "There is no home for them to return to. There is nothing behind them except for fire, smoke and rubble. Burning death. All they have is the path before them, the book that they seek, that song that we've all heard so much about for so many years. Even the little one, Mara knows of the Litany. She seems to know the tune of it, the melody and harmony. She cannot sing the words though. She hums this unearthly tune while she walks along with a smile on her lips and in her eyes. It's as though the words are inside of her and she knows them secretly. She bottles them up away from the world, and she's a tough little nut that won't be easily cracked."

Brother Demen looked at Mara, sleeping in Anomalie's lap. "So innocent, that child. What a sad tale that she is living." He stared at her for a long moment.

Sigil broke the silence, "We can *change* her tale, brother. But to achieve that, we need power. We need to find Engineer, and quickly."

"Yes, yes. So you do, it seems." The priest stood and pushed in his chair. "Wait here. I will call for my brother, the one who knew Engineer. Please, get some rest and take what food you need from the cabinets. I will return soon." And he turned and went out the way they came in. To Anomalie, it seemed as if the shadows cast on the wall shifted slightly, and then he was gone.

He returned in no more than an hour with another hooded monk in tow. Anomalie had been dozing on a cushioned chair with Mara in her lap and was startled awake by their sudden appearance. As always, Sigil was awake.

"This is Brother Samael," said Demen, as the monk entered the sacristy and bowed. "He will tell you what he can about Engineer."

"I am very glad to see you, Brother Sigil. And Mara as well. It is as if a dream is coming true," said Samael as he took the chair that Sigil offered. He declined the offer of food and drink and began to speak.

"Engineer was born in the Crax, as was I. Our childhood was very difficult, as is the childhood of everyone born in such a place. Engineer was very different from the rest of us. He could see things, in his mind, that we could not."

Sigil and Anomalie were both listening intently. He continued.

"I tell you this as a warning, Sigil. Engineer could always be dangerous. He is very intelligent, but dangerous. He has never been afraid; he was always seeking knowledge even if it meant much risk to his life. Or the lives of others." He paused to see if his words were affecting them. When he saw that they did not flinch, he shook his head and went on. "Very well. I cannot tell you where Engineer is. His comings and goings are always secretive. But he is close to the children of the Crax. They will be able to lead you to him."

"The children?" questioned Sigil.

"The children of the Crax are very isolated. They take to the night apart from their elders, and live in gangs, roaming. Most cannot read or write in the traditional sense, they gather information directly from the streets, using a pidgin slang. I myself would have never learned, had it not been for the Order. But Engineer somehow learned on his own. Not only to read and write in standard Judicial English, but he became fluent in many ancient languages. No one knows how he accomplished it, because, as you know, after the Culture war, many of those languages were suppressed or stamped out. But somehow, he did. There are rumors that he teaches some of the children in the gangs. If this is so, and I believe that it is, there will be children in the Crax that can tell you how to contact him."

Sigil nodded. "Understood. Then how will we find these children?" he asked.

Brother Samael lifted his eyes abruptly. "Fret not. If you enter the Crax again, and move about for long enough, the children will find you."

Sigil nodded again and thanked both of the priests. Although the priests made a final protest and warning to them, Sigil assured them that all would be well. The monks bade them a doubtful farewell. Mara was waking, and Sigil got to his feet, gesturing to Anomalie to do the same. She set Mara down and held her hand. Together they prepared to return to the Crax, and Engineer.

Chapter 12

Wetware

Of their connection with Engineer
and of the puzzle of Anomalie's blood

THEY STOOD together on the street outside the subway station. Sigil and Anomalie stared in both directions down the long avenues as Mara kicked her feet through the snow, making soft puffs.

"I think we should go back and get the car," said Anomalie.

"For what reason? We can't move quietly with the car," replied Sigil. He looked across the park, where their footprints had already been covered by the falling snow.

"Why be quiet?" she returned. "We're *trying* to be found aren't we? Plus, Engineer said that he would contact us at some point. Why not just hide out somewhere and wait?"

"Brother Samael said that the children would find us if we moved around the Crax," he answered. "I assumed that they have been tracking us for the entire time that we've been here. I thought that we would be more easily approached on foot."

"Maybe that's true, but the car is easier to spot..." she muttered.

"Anomalie. Just say it," said Sigil.

"Well, I really like that car!" she blurted out. "I mean, it's crazy. It's a real old-school hot-rod!" She held her hands out to her side in explanation. "It's just that I've never seen anything like that before. It would be a waste to just leave it in an alley somewhere." She had a sheepish expression on her face. "Mara likes it too." she added, looking down at Mara for support.

"Is that true, Mara?" asked Sigil. "What's your opinion?"

Mara had taken the cue from Anomalie. "The car is super cool!" she said. She did like the car, but more importantly, she sensed that it would make Anomalie happy. It was the first time that she'd disagreed with Sigil.

Sigil laughed. "Fine then. You're right. I cannot think of a real reason not to at least get out of the weather. Back to the car it is."

Anomalie only nodded in agreement, but he could see a small smile of victory on her face. She reached down to squeeze Mara's hand as they began to make their way back the way they had come.

They crossed cautiously through the park again, aware that they were probably being watched. As they passed through the gate of the park, and began to make their way along the sidewalk, Sigil stopped abruptly, holding his fist near the side of his head to halt them. They froze.

"What's up?" Anomalie whispered, peering forward through the hazy, dim glow of the streetlights.

"A person. Near the car," Sigil said in a low voice. They could not quite see the car; they had hidden it just slightly inside a small alley, but Sigil seemed certain. The muzzle of his rifle rose and he looked over his sights, peering into the fog.

"What do we do?" Anomalie asked.

Sigil only paused for a heartbeat before answering. "We go forward," he said.

They walked slowly toward the space where they had left the car, Sigil taking the lead with Mara between them. When they turned the corner of the alley, they saw a strange sight. Sitting on top of the hood of the car was a boy, no older than thirteen or fourteen years of age. He was dressed in a bulky, quilted winter coat and baggy trousers. His hair was thrown upward in a shock of spiky tufts and folded partially down underneath the strap of a set of huge headphones. His eyes were covered with goggles that looked like they had once belonged to an ancient aviator, except the glossy lenses had an orange tint. When he saw them, he reached up and pulled his headphones down around his neck and slid from the hood of the car.

"Oiisse!" he grunted. "You be da rokkers I sent to fetch, neh? One guy, two chicks, neh?" Ignoring Sigil's rifle, he sauntered towards them, but stopped when he saw Anomalie tense and Sigil subdue her with his outstretched arm.

"Who are you?" asked Sigil, lowering his rifle.

"I? I is *Tobi* yo neh. Toe…bee…I am wit Too/Sicks Crew." He looked from Sigil to Anomalie and saw that they didn't recognize the reference. "From two block, six street neh? You no grok it?" They cast blank stares at him. He sucked his teeth in exasperation and pointed at the Coupe. "Here is Engineer's tech, no? He sent I to fetch da car and da three rokkers wid it. One guy, two chicks, neh. So here I be."

"You know where Engineer is now?" asked Sigil.

"*So* yo neh! I said it two time now. I sent to fetch you and da car. Bring you to Engineer's lab." Tobi started to walk back to the driver's side door. "You comin'?" he said over his shoulder. Sigil and Anomalie looked at each other.

"That was quick," she said under her breath.

Sigil nodded and led the way. "It *is* his car," he said. "He must be tracking it. Good call on coming back for it." They got in the car after Tobi, Sigil in the passenger seat and Mara and Anomalie behind. Tobi put the car into gear and pulled it out onto the street.

They drove in silence until they reached a part of the Crax where the buildings were no more than fallen skeletons, their framing and wiring exposed. The streetlights became fewer until, finally, there was only moonlight and the car's headlights to show their way.

Anomalie's voice broke the silence. "Hey. Tobi. Can you answer a question for me?" she asked.

"So yo. Send it. If I know it, I answer," he said, without taking his eyes off of the road.

"How come it's snowing in the Crax? I mean, if we're underground? And how come I can see the moon and stars?" She was looking out the window as she asked, to make sure that she wasn't mistaken about that last fact.

"That Engineer's tech too. It always snowin' down here. Engineer send wifi direct to da headgear. To everybody. It jack up you brainspace. So da Crews can hide. It not really real, neh? You grok?"

"Yea," she whispered to herself, and nodded. "I grok it." Tobi turned over his shoulder to grin at her, then turned back to the street. Anomalie thought about what he had said. Somehow, Engineer was creating a huge virtual reality grid down here in the Crax. She was not a trained technician but she had some idea of how much energy that would take. And how sophisticated the software would necessarily be. All of that, just to make it easier for some gang kids to hide. She thought back to Meeko and Walter, the two synth AIs that they had met at Engineer's workshop, and looked down at the stone hanging from her neck. It was mind boggling and a bit frightening to think of what Engineer might be capable of. But it was exciting to her, too. She laughed inwardly when she remembered how scared the priest at the church looked when she had just *mentioned* Engineer. Nothing made her happier than scaring authority figures like that. If Engineer was able to put a look like that on an old priest's face, she definitely couldn't wait to meet this guy.

Tobi pulled the Coupe into a side street and turned off the headlights. They drove straight for a while in the inky darkness. Anomalie scanned ahead and could see that Tobi was driving perfectly fine. She glanced at him and saw some tiny icons flickering in his goggles. She figured that he probably had better implants than she did. Even here in the Crax, her gear was outclassed. After a while, they reached a large garage door at the end of the dead-end. Tobi slowly came to a stop and idled the car until the door lifted open, pouring light out into the street. Tobi lifted his foot off the clutch, and the Coupe rolled inside.

Immediately, Anomalie's electronics overloaded. Her HUD was filled with white noise and crackled off. She nearly panicked until she realized that her gyros were still operating; she swiveled her head back and forth to confirm it. She reached up and tapped Sigil on the shoulder.

"Something in here's messing with my sensors," she warned. He nodded and opened his door. She did the same and motioned for Mara to follow her out on the same side. Tobi swung himself out as well, and they were greeted by a loud voice.

"Back here! I am in the process of taking samples..." The voice trailed away.

"Engineer yo neh. Da force wid da source, neh?" Tobi tossed his head in the direction of the back, and walked in that direction. Sigil, Anomalie and Mara followed.

They passed a series of tall, metal storage cabinets and entered a large laboratory. Inside the lab, with his back to them, was a towering, heavy-set man in a long lab coat, his hair pulled back into a braided ponytail that fell nearly to his waist. The man had been busy, bent over a workbench, but he turned and faced them as they filed into the room. He had a massive graying beard that reached to the center of his chest and his eyes, focusing on them from behind steel-rimmed spectacles, were sharp and piercing.

"Greetings and salutations, Sigil. I apologize for the crossed wires earlier, and for heading your message off at the pass, so to speak. I would have liked to have met you at my primary workshop. But, as you know, that location was compromised." He walked forward and held out his hand to Sigil. Sigil hesitated, eyeing Engineer's face. Then, reluctantly coming to a decision, he slowly lifted his arm and shook Engineer's hand.

"Engineer, I presume?" said Sigil.

Engineer smiled wryly. "Yes, I am Engineer."

"Do you always read mail that is not addressed to you?" asked Sigil, with a raised eyebrow.

"I *have* been known to read things not intended for my eyes from time to time, yes," he answered. "I assumed that I would be more useful to you, upon your arrival, than those arrogant monks you seem to be so attached to. I also assumed that you could be useful to me." His tone changed, became oblique. "I'm sure you've heard a few things about me since you've arrived. I'm afraid that some of it is probably true." Both Sigil and Anomalie nodded.

Engineer chuckled, mostly to himself. "Rumors have a way of growing exponentially, but there is some fact to them." He noticed Mara and changed the topic. "This is the child that came through with you?" he asked Sigil.

"Yes. This is Mara Worth. She is under my protection," answered Sigil. "For what that is worth..." he finished.

"Hello Mara," said Engineer kindly, leaning forward and holding his hand out to her. She shyly took it and he gave a slight shake. "I understand that you are a very special girl. Do you like the stone that I gave you?" Mara nodded with a small smile, but she lowered her eyes and moved closer to Anomalie's leg. Anomalie put her hand on top of Mara's head protectively.

"And you are?" said Engineer to Anomalie, looking first at the anchor hanging from her neck and then lifting his eyes to meet hers. She set her jaw stubbornly and met his eyes with as much courage as she could manage.

"I'm Anomalie. Anomalie Harper. I'm with them," she said firmly.

Engineer seemed to be looking closely at Anomalie's eyes. She was still for a moment, but then fidgeted uncomfortably under his inspection. She realized that he wasn't studying her eyes, but was looking inside of her eyes, perhaps checking for discoloration or distention from former implanting procedures. Then, he moved to her ears, cocking his head slightly, before moving down and closely inspecting the rest of her body. When he reached her waist, she turned sideways, appearing slightly dismayed.

"Hey! Are you looking for something special there?" she said hotly.

Engineer glanced sharply upward, back to her face. "Actually, I was. Looking for something special, as you say..." He looked back to address Sigil.

"She did not come through with Mara and yourself, correct? The Label satellite would have relayed such a huge energy delta. I would have known." He hurried to a computer interface at a nearby workstation and made a few deft movements. Software began to load on the screen.

Sigil shook his head. "No, she did not. When we moved between eras, it was only the two of us. I was separated from Mara in transit. When I awoke in this era, Anomalie found me and assisted me. Then she joined us. She has been with us since," he said, watching Engineer as he moved about the laboratory. Engineer was a flurry of activity, switching on equipment and computers, marking notes on various notebooks that were strewn across the benches. He went to a rack of equipment and took what looked to be a bulky handgun with a wrist thick barrel from it. He stretched a cable from a device on a bench to the gun and plugged it into the gun's handgrip. Then he casually aimed it at Anomalie.

"Whoa, whoa, whoa! What did *I* do?" exclaimed Anomalie, shocked. She was a single breath away from sprinting full-speed toward Engineer to defend herself when he held up a hand to pacify them.

"Don't worry. It's only a scope. To check your implants," he explained, and pulled the trigger. They slowly relaxed. Nothing happened visibly, but Anomalie could sense the scope scanning her. She stood still and was reminded of her last visit to a doctor's office. She saw Tobi staring at her from the corner of the lab and she glared at him. He ignored it and continued to stare. Engineer was staring down at the readout on the scope. He switched his eyes from the scope to the device that it was plugged into, comparing the differences. He switched off the scope.

"Well?" said Anomalie. "My 'plants aren't working in here anyway. My HUD crashed as soon as we pulled the car inside."

Engineer nodded absently, studying the data he'd collected. His eyes scanning a nearby screen, he lowered himself into the chair in front of it. "Right. That's right. This lab is cloaked from outside electronic peeking. Like a Faraday cage, but made of..." His voice trailed off as he looked more closely at the screen. "Holy..." he whispered to himself.

"What?" said Anomalie, embarrassed. "I know that they're low gen. I don't come from money or anything. I just have the basic package." She noticed Engineer's expression and she started to worry. She went to where he sat viewing the screen and looked over his shoulder anxiously. "Seriously. What?"

Engineer stroked his beard, fingering his chin in concentration as he considered the data. His eyes closed as his head tipped back and he leaned back into his chair. Anomalie looked worriedly at Sigil but he shrugged at her, not knowing what to make of Engineer's reaction.

"What's wrong with me? I mean, beyond outdated, crashed 'plants?" she pleaded. Engineer opened his eyes and came to a decision.

"I'd like to do a blood test." He looked at Anomalie for a response. She looked at Sigil again for support. Sigil walked over to where Anomalie stood and put his arm on her shoulder and looked squarely at Engineer.

"For what reason?" he asked. He was willing to let Engineer do whatever was required; he knew that the summoning had already been invasive enough. But he also recognized Anomalie's nervousness and knew that she needed his confirmation.

"I think I can fix your implants," said Engineer. "Actually, I know that I can."

"What do you mean, fix?" asked Anomalie. "Most of my gear is really old-school. Some of it is bootlegged off the street, so it was junk when I got it. I don't want anyone that I don't know digging into my skull..."

"No. You're wrong," replied Engineer. "Let me guess, you get odd glitches when the grids are high-traffic. But, the glitches come in a rhythmic pattern, correct? Sometimes, they get faster, the pace increases and then just stops. Is this right?"

Anomalie nodded, but was still skeptical. "Sure, but that's just bandwidth flutter as the server receivers sync with the sats. Once they come into phase, I'm all good."

"But you also get intermittent interference even when you're offline, I bet. Nothing networked and yet you have lags between your head and your joints. Ring a bell?"

She frowned but nodded again. "So what? So I'm busted. Like I said, junk 'plants."

Engineer shook his head again and pointed to the display. "Like *I* said. You're wrong. You don't have a hardware problem, you have a software problem. Even if you had the most current gen implants, you would still have the same bugs. I can easily upgrade your hardware. And I don't even have to dig into you to do it. Well...not much." He smiled and she gave him a dirty look.

"There is something in your blood that is affecting your software," he finished.

She looked at him blankly, not understanding. "My blood?" she questioned.

"Yes. I think that the composition of your blood is causing your software to glitch. I've seen this before actually," he said, pushing back the chair and rising to his feet.

"Like a disease or something?" she asked, "Am I sick? I feel fine..."

"I don't think so, not a disease. But I will have to take a blood sample and run some more tests to be sure. If I'm right, I think I can make it so that you won't ever have problems with your gear again."

Anomalie couldn't imagine it. Ever since she could remember, she had always been behind everyone else because of her 'plants. Studying was harder for her, sports were harder for her. She had only been able to keep up at all by bypassing her software and doing things manually. When others had been able to rely on the data from the network during exams or games, she had often been forced to expect the worst: a gray out, or even a data black out. When she was a young child, it had confused and terrified her, like being suddenly blinded. But she had compensated. She studied longer hours, read things manually instead of scanning them. She exercised instead of simply loading sports apps into her servos, but none of it had worked. Each year she'd fallen further and further behind until eventually, she was entirely out of the loop. After that, it had only been her and Colleen. And they had both known that they really didn't have much of a future.

But now, Engineer was telling her that he could fix it, fix her. He could change it so that she was just like everyone else, always connected to the net, with a connection that could be relied on.

She nodded, too excited to speak, in case she broke the spell. Engineer pointed to a door at the side of the laboratory.

"Come with me. I have a test suite set up in there. We can run the blood samples and I can check out your implants more closely." He began to walk toward the testing room. Anomalie glanced at Sigil and he gave her a look of encouragement. Still worried, but with heady anticipation, she followed Engineer into the testing room.

Once inside, he gestured toward a large reclining chair with comfortable looking armrests. Anomalie climbed into it and waited. Engineer began to switch on various devices, preparing to test her. When the devices were ready, he told her to hold out her arm.

"This will pinch a little…" he said. She nodded and swallowed. He inserted a small plasticine port into a vein, then used multiple syringes to take a set of blood samples. He went to a small cooler box and removed a vial containing a chemical and added it to one of the samples. Inserting that sample into a centrifuge, he turned it on. The other samples went into devices that Anomalie didn't recognize at all.

"The blood samples will take some time," said Engineer. "While we wait, I'd like to scope your implant system again." Anomalie watched as he inserted a long tube into the port in her arm. "I'm injecting a chemical that will make it easier for me to trace your circuitry visually with the scope. You will feel a cold sensation and then it will become very hot for about 15 seconds, got it?" She nodded, he turned a small valve on the tube, and she watched as the chemical flowed into her arm. Just as Engineer said, she felt the cold and then the heat, and then it leveled out and she felt a little numb.

Engineer reclined the chair fully and swung a flat screen on a swiveled arm over her head. "I'll begin with your head, and move down as I trace. You okay?" he asked.

She nodded. "Will it hurt?" she asked. She had memories of painful implant procedures that she had endured when she was very young and still growing rapidly.

"Not at all. You can speak and even move around a bit while I work. I'll keep up with the trace. I'm pretty good at this you know," he said with a smile.

She smiled nervously but nodded. "Okay, I'm ready," she said.

"Okay, here we go then," said Engineer as he started the circuit trace.

While he worked, Anomalie's mind began to churn. She turned the images of the Archons over and over again, trying to make sense of them and of Sigil and Mara. She had seen so many bizarre things since she had joined them; it was beginning to take its toll on her. She thought of Engineer as the same as her. He knew science, and computing, and tech. But, most importantly, he was from her time and he spoke as if he was from the grids. She ventured to seek some clarity from him.

"Those two outside, Sigil and Mara. You know them?" she started.

Engineer continued to look at the screen and at other instruments that lined the wall when he answered, "Not really. I had read about Sigil. I knew a bit of his history. I knew about the Fall, and the Fall of the Abbey." He shifted the screen away from her and attached some small electrodes to the implant ports on the sides of her neck, just below her ears. He switched on another machine and moved the screen back into place above her. "That particular myth was especially hard to come by."

"So it's not true, the story that they're telling. It's only a myth. They haven't come from the past?" she said, with a tone of near relief.

"No, it's definitely true. They are from the past. Quite a while in the past actually. Sigil especially has arrived from a very long time ago." He chuckled again to himself in the strange way that he had.

"How do you know?" she asked, but she already suspected his answer.

"I brought them here," he replied. "From the past. Using something similar to the summoning program that you are so intimately familiar with." Anomalie leaned back and looked at the ceiling as he spoke. He sighed. "In order to explain it clearly, I have to start with the Label."

The term was familiar to her, she had heard it a number of times since she had met Sigil and Mara. "Yes. What is this Label that I keep hearing about."

"It's a satellite. A military intelligence satellite. But it was stolen. And then I stole it from the people who had stolen it originally." There was a blank stare on Anomalie's face. "I was able to reverse engineer the temporal merge system from data that I found on a rogue satellite," he said.

"Rogue?" said Anomalie. "What do you mean, rogue?"

"When I was doing independent sweeps of telecommunication equipment, back before I left the Crax for the Judicial Grids, I discovered a satellite. The satellite was moving in a strange way, a way that couldn't possibly be accounted for by predictable celestial mechanics. The trajectory that it took appeared as a typical ellipse, but then it would vanish. Then it would reappear, some time later, and the trajectory would describe a different, unrelated ellipse. It was really weird."

"Yea, really weird," said Anomalie, not completely following.

"So, I pondered it for a while. A long while, actually. Then, one day, it dawned on me. The various ellipses made sense, if they were chained together. They described a single, larger ellipse, but only if the satellite was actually traveling on a path that was far different than it appeared visually. I tried a number of different mathematics: quaternions, relativistic, various vector schemes, none of it worked. But then..."

"Then?" said Anomalie, picking up on his obvious excitement.

"Then, it really hit me!" he exclaimed, poking his finger into the air triumphantly. "The path of the satellite made sense if it was not only moving through space but also showing variation in time!"

"The satellite was traveling through time?" she said, skeptically.

"Just a bit. Actually, it was oscillating forward and backward in time. So, I cracked it. I was able to side-load some of my own code onto the satellite and brute force the encryption. What I found then *really* blew my mind."

"What did you find?" prompted Anomalie, excited in spite of herself.

"There was a message. From years ago, encoded into the data that I found. See, the satellite was originally part of a military project, code-named 'Label'. It seems that, at the start of the Culture War, the satellite had been hacked and used by the resistance to store data and to be something like a remote control station for their network. An off-planet headquarters for intel, comm, information based material, get it?"

She nodded. "But what was the message?" she asked.

"I'm getting to that," he replied. "I couldn't read the message, but I knew it was there. I've seen a lot of code in my time, a lot of languages. I can tell if something is a language, even if it doesn't seem like one at first glance, you know?"

She did know. She'd done her own share of hacking and understood that all languages had similarities, patterns that repeated or would emerge upon deeper inspection. It was cryptography 101. She nodded.

"But this language was different. It had texture to it."

"Texture?"

"Yes, like something tactile. Or maybe sensory is a better word. It had a beauty to it. It took me a number of years to decode it. In the end, I found that the key to decrypting it was music." He moved to another position so that he could get a better reading from his scan. At the mention of music, Anomalie focused more intently.

"How did you use music to crack it?" she asked.

"I didn't *use* music, it *was* music. The language, I mean. It was music made of light."

"Wha-a-a-t...?" she drawled slowly, not understanding at all.

"I finally found that the language itself, the characters of the alphabet, the numerals, the grammar, everything, could be expressed like musical scales, but at an extremely high frequency. In the light spectrum. Once I had that math, I could read the message."

Anomalie was unable to wrap her head around what Engineer was saying, but she was intrigued. Engineer's story had hooked her. "But, what did it say? The message." she asked again.

"Oh that. Right." he replied. "It was from Sigil, requesting evac. In a language called Angelic. But he didn't need to be picked up from a place. He and Mara needed to be picked up from time. From a 'temporal merge' I believe is the official, technical term. The message was meant for some religious group called The Order of Dismas, but I got to it first and kept the satellite, which I now use for *my* work. Spoils of war and all that," he finished.

"But, how is that possible, them moving throughout time like that?" She still wanted to understand, her brain was grasping at what Engineer was describing.

Engineer paused and stroked his chin. After some consideration, he tried to explain. "Have you ever had a memory enter into your mind that you weren't sure was true? Something that you might have seen in a vid or had read in a story? I once had a memory resurface in my mind of a party that I had been at. I was watching a vid and there was a scene of a very wealthy party. The party was held at a lavish mansion, the lawns and gardens were luxurious and expansive; the party-goers were exquisitely dressed.

"The scene in the vid immediately triggered for me, a memory of a party that I had actually witnessed. In my memory of it, there were certain distinctive occurrences. There was a very attractive woman wearing a stylish dress, the fact that the host was wealthy enough to have purchased special wines and beers was clear to me. I could see the property that the party was held on spread out before me. I thought of this gala and, within a few moments, I realized that I had never been to this place.

"This didn't bother me, I assumed that I had seen it in another vid. But, the moment that I thought about the initial vid, I knew that I was mistaken. I was very certain that this party scene was not from a fictional story or a propaganda spin. I thought about it for perhaps a week and started to wonder if I had only dreamed it. It was so very clear to me! I could see the wine arrayed on the tables, I could see the special kegs of beer. I could clearly see the woman with the unique dress. I could even picture the foods that had been served. I vaguely wondered about it for a few days before I fell asleep and suddenly it popped into my mind as I awoke.

"This party was a party that had been described to me by a friend who had attended it. I was shocked. I had never even seen this place at all, it had all been described to me verbally, during a conversation. Somehow, I had visualized this party so clearly, when my friend was discussing it, that the memory of the visualization had been interpreted, years later, as one of my own. I realized that our memories can often be faulty."

Anomalie nodded. "I've read things about witnesses to accidents and crimes having bogus memories when they're questioned by the Judies," she said.

Engineer went on. "Exactly. Who's to say that our dreams can't even be interpreted as real? It's totally probable that you would know that a dream wasn't real, if the dream was of something *unreal* or fantastic. If you dreamed that you were flying above a pink castle made of toffee, you wouldn't think it was real, but what if you dreamed that you had woken up, went to your kitchen and made some toast? It would be very difficult to decide if that had happened in reality or not, no?"

Anomalie looked at him impatiently. "So what does this have to do with time travel?" she prodded.

He held up a hand. "I'm getting to that, calm down." He went on. "What I mean is that much of what happens in the past is a sum product of many stories, from many different sources. Think about it, there are a series of credible sources for history. Textbooks and school sources, oral accounts, witness accounts, propa spins and so on, right? There are also bizarre stories, fairy tales, myths, legends and religious dogma. In the credible sources, there must be things that are fabricated... false, right?" Anomalie nodded. "And in the myths, fairy tales and religious stories, there might be events that actually happened, correct?" She nodded again.

"So, if we consider that and factor in the fact that our own individual memories may actually be compiled from dreams, fantasies or stories that we heard from others, mashed together with a biased interpretation of actual events, it means that the past, history, is nothing more than fiction." He paused and waited for her response. Her eyes drifted upwards as she considered it.

"Go on..." she said.

"Okay, so this holds true for each individual person who is experiencing the sensation of memory. Not only is memory fictional, but every person's idea of the past is both entirely fictional and completely different from everybody else's. Now, hold onto that thought and we'll move onto the perception of the future." She squinted at him.

"Well, most people hold to the idea that the future is unknowable. Time moves forward in a linear path from the past, through the present and into the future. Events unravel in a defined direction. We can use our memory to look into and examine our past, but we can't look into the future and know anything concretely, right?"

He didn't stop to notice her response. He was warming to the subject. "But often, man speculates about the future and builds a definite vision of it. For example, imagine a man who lived around 1800, who witnessed the first steam locomotive. The man is mightily impressed with such a great innovation and he correctly surmises that, one day, man will even have inventions that will allow him to fly or harness electricity to process information. He can even picture it in his mind. If he were to say, at that present moment, that those things would come to pass, would he be saying an untruth? Others around him would claim that it was impossible to know such things, but he would have been correct. Could he say that he KNOWS it?

"Conversely, imagine a person with strong religious beliefs. They can make statements about the future such as, 'There will be a second coming of the Messiah.', or 'We will go to Heaven after we die.' Scientifically minded people will say, 'That is not true, you are only basing it on a belief.' But is it any different from the steam locomotive enthusiast who 'believes' that computers will be created? How is his sense of being 'right' any stronger than that of religious faith? So we establish that the future is also fictional, but sometimes laced with elements of fact. Are you with me so far?" She was concentrating intently on what he was saying. He continued.

"In actuality, both the past and the future are works of fiction, products of the mind's power of perception to create a matrix of potentials. Some of these potentials form into physical phenomenon on this planet. There is only *one* past, made up of an oscillating ratio of truth and fantasy. Let's call this the Fable era."

"The Fable era..." repeated Anomalie.

"Yes, the Fable era is this strange period that seems to exist before the current experience. It is created out of a mixture of likely past events and arising memories and is subjectively unique for each observer. Also, there is only one future. Let's call this the Potential era. This is a speculative state that each individual creates for himself or herself out of hopes, ambitions, fears and faith. Understand?"

"The Potential era and the Fable era."

"Yes, for some, the Fable era is filled with magic and gods; for others, wars and plagues. Neither is true in an objective, testable sense. The Potential era is also created of two opposing views. For some, it's made of technological advancements and scientific discoveries, for others, it arises out of prophecies and desires. Once again, neither is true in a way that can be tested or proven. But, it gets even weirder..." He smiled.

"Okay, hit me," she said, rolling her eyes.

"There is a third period of time. The present, which I'll call for the sake of this discussion, The Gray Mundane. This is the era where the consciousness interacts with matter and the mind experiences the world in its present state. The Now." He knocked his knuckles against the wooden workbench to emphasize his point. "The Angelic race can move freely between all three eras. This is why you were able to encounter Sigil, who is a product of the Fable era and Mara who experiences the Gray Mundane, here in what can be termed the Potential era."

"But that makes no sense! This seems to be the present to me." she exclaimed. Engineer held up a hand to stop her.

"Not so. *This* is an era with no thread into the future. The Monarchy has been aggressive in destroying any creative work that can instill hope or imagination in the masses. Destroy hope, destroy the future potential.

"The moment that you began moving with Sigil and Mara, you became ensnared into their experience. Sigil is aware of all three eras, and Mara is also perceiving this as a potential future. Now that you can also move between the three eras, this epoch will always manifest in the world as the fulfillment of potentials. This is the actual future. Not a potential dream or fear, but the realization of dreams and fears.

"To a Christian, it would be as if Armageddon had occurred, to a Buddhist it would mean that the wheel of karma had stopped turning for all living creatures; to a computer scientist, it is the technological singularity or the birth of true, strong AI. That is what has actually occurred. Armageddon is here, the angels are in combat. Karma has stopped, there is no cause and effect. This *is* the singularity, the end of hope for the future.

"Think of it this way, human beings can move laterally through space but can only move in one direction through time. They move from the past into the future but can walk in any direction through a room or on a map, right? Now imagine a tree. A tree is alive but can only move through time and only in one direction. The tree can grow somewhat but can not move laterally. It lives out its entire existence in a reasonably stationary state. If a tree was conscious and could perceive animal life, it would seem that there was a higher degree of movement that it could not attain. The Angelic race moves freely through time and perceives humanity in the way that we perceive trees. By moving and associating your movement with Sigil and Mara, you have attained that higher degree of movement."

Engineer made some adjustments to one of the machines beside him. "There was a twentieth century author, Philip K. Dick—" he began.

"Yea," interjected Anomalie, "Blade Runner, right? That's one of my favorite vids. I read *Do Androids Dream of Electric Sheep?* and *Flow My Tears, the Policeman Said*, too."

"Really?" replied Engineer, impressed. "How did you possibly procure that material? It's highly illegal, you know."

"How did you crack that satellite? And learn how to read that scribbly code?" she responded.

"Touché," said Engineer. "But, back to my point. P.K. Dick had a number of theories, some of which he explored in his works, that pointed to the fact that he was not actually living in the time that he was experiencing. That his perception of time and reality was actually a cover, or veil, over the reality underlying it. Follow?"

"I think so," said Anomalie.

"As a matter of fact, Dick had an experience, related to the book you mentioned, *Flow My Tears*, that I believe was his peering through that veil."

Anomalie thought about what she remembered from the book, but didn't understand. Engineer looked up, and saw her brow knotted from confusion and went on.

"I'll explain more to you when we have more time," he assured her, "but for now, just know that P.K. Dick was right, not crazy, and I figured out a way to exploit that fact."

There was a beep from one of the machines and Engineer spun his chair to face it. He reached into a small compartment on the machine and removed one of the vials of Anomalie's blood. He put it into a stand on the bench next to the machine. Then, he sat for a long while, studying the results of the test as they scrolled across the screen on the machine.

"What is it?" asked Anomalie.

"It's exactly as I suspected," he answered, and tapped a button to print. The printout began to churn out of the bottom of another machine. "Your blood has certain emergent properties that makes it superior to even Sigil's for the Archon technology. This is unbelievable..."

"What does that mean? I can summon Archons, too?" she wondered aloud.

"No, you can't. But, I wasn't sure if the Archons would even sync with someone without angelic blood. I assumed that you would be rejected by either the Archon or the system itself." Anomalie looked at him with derision. "Don't take it personally!" he shot back. "I had never run the system before. But I was certain that Sigil could handle it because he had encountered an anchor in the past. The legend references it. I also thought that anyone that could move through time with him would be fine, so Mara would be okay. You were another matter." He spun the chair back to face her. "It seems that your blood is a new thing entirely."

"New? Like, my blood isn't normal? That's just great, another oddball thing about me." She looked angry.

"No! You don't understand. There are electro-chemical properties that are apparent in your tests, showing that you may be able to sync even more completely with the Archon than any other being that's been studied. I'm not sure exactly how it has developed, but your numbers are off the chart on my compatibility scans. It's as if my software was modeled specifically on your DNA. It's bizarre..." he said as his eyes went back to the data.

"So that's why my 'plants have never worked right?" she asked.

"Precisely. I can adjust your operating system and bionics to account for the new numbers from your blood and you should be right as rain. Also, I can make a few non-invasive tweaks to your hardware that can even enhance your performance. What do you think?" He looked at her.

It didn't take her more than a second to decide. "Go for it, Doc. Patch my system." A wide smile spread across her face.

He nodded and turned back to the workbench, but before he moved again, there was a loud crash from the laboratory outside. The testing room went dark and then became flooded in the red light of the auxiliary generator. They heard Mara's voice cry out.

"Mara!" exclaimed Anomalie, and leaped from the chair, pulling the electrodes and IV port from her skin. She rushed into the laboratory with Engineer following at her heels. They saw Sigil lying on the floor, not moving. Anomalie searched throughout the lab, but Mara and Tobi were nowhere to be found.

Chapter 13

Stolen

*Of The Taking of Mara
and of Solomon's Revenge*

ANOMALIE rushed to Sigil's side; he was conscious but in a thick daze. He looked up at her as if peering through a dense fog, and tried to struggle to his feet. He fell back heavily to the floor, unable to speak.

"What happened? Where's Mara? And that Crax kid?" She spun her head to glare at Engineer. "If your kid did anything to her, I'll rip you apart. Tell me where they are," she demanded.

Engineer was typing furiously at a keyboard, his fingers a blur. "Tobi set off a fork-bomb in the system. I may be able to stop it from fragging everything." He paused and turned back to Anomalie. "I'm sorry. I didn't see this coming. Tobi surprised me, too. I had no idea that he figured this system out." He went on with his typing, trying to stem the flood of processes that were eating his computer system.

"A fork-bomb? How could a tacky virus like that knock Sigil down. There's no way that little punk could have taken both of them. Or even Mara by herself." She helped Sigil to his feet as he began to shake off the effects of Tobi's attack.

"This system is set up to run code in a language called Angelic script," explained Engineer. "It's the language that I used in the summoning programs. It's like a language that the angels use to manipulate matter and energy. Tobi must have figured out a way to hack it. He used a drop-in to send an interference signal directly to your friends' nervous systems; it would have stunned them and caused them to black out. Then he ran the fork-bomb to burn the whole system. Luckily, I caught it in time."

"We must go after her..." said Sigil weakly, fighting through his confusion and leaning on Anomalie for support.

"We will," said Engineer. "But it will take me some time to get the system back online. He took my car. He's probably disabled the primary tracking system, but there are other ways for me to track it." He was moving rapidly around the lab, resetting and re-calibrating the equipment. The main lights came on with a loud noise; the hum of servers and other electronics once again began to fill the lab.

"Then do it!" shouted Anomalie. She turned to Sigil. "Are you going to be alright?" she asked.

He nodded. "I will be fine. The boy's attack was enough to knock us down but not to injure me. Mara was certainly not harmed by it. But, he may be taking her to people who *can* harm her. We must move quickly."

As they prepared to follow Tobi and Mara, Anomalie paced restlessly, like a caged cat, impatient.

"Why is this taking so long?" she erupted. "That little girl is alone out there. With some sort of Judicial monster. We have to go now!"

"I'm nearly finished," said Engineer. "I have another vehicle that we can use to follow them. I only need to gather a few more pieces of equipment." He started toward the rear of the laboratory but Anomalie ran to intercept him.

"I'll watch you," she said. "I don't trust you. How do we know that you didn't tell your kid to take her?" she said accusingly as she let him pass. She fell into step alongside of him.

"I understand how you feel, but I assure you that I didn't. Tobi is a very troubled child, like every child from the Crax. I'll find out why he did this. But, my goals are the same as yours. You must try to trust me," he said.

"Why should we?" she insisted.

"You have no choice!" exploded Engineer, stopping in his tracks and staring hard at her. "All of what you see, or hear, or feel in the Crax is generated by my system. The code that is bonding the Archons to you is generated by my system. The very procedure that brought that little girl here was developed by me! You must trust that I would not bring her here to simply hand her over to the Monarchy. Do you understand?" He was breathing heavily, and his face was red.

Anomalie froze, recognizing real concern in Engineer's face. Slowly, she nodded. "But you don't know her. You haven't seen what she can do. They'll kill her if they can," she said, tension rising in her voice.

Engineer nodded, took a deep breath and tried to calm her. He began to remove various small electronic devices from the shelves and put them into a satchel as he spoke. "I can only imagine that her power is beyond what either of us can understand. If the Monarchy wants her that badly, then there is some reason for it, and that's reason enough for me to want to stop them."

She didn't have an answer for that, so she stayed silent as he filled his satchel with the last pieces of equipment. Finally, he looked up.

"I'm ready. My car is this way. Let's go." he said. He led the way to a back door of the building, where another car was waiting outside. He moved to the driver's door as they got in on the opposite side. They drove away from the laboratory and entered the maze of the Crax.

Sigil, still recovering from Tobi's attack, questioned Engineer as he drove. "Why did you begin to fight the Monarchy?" he asked.

Engineer considered the question before he answered, "Some of the days that I spent in the grids were good. Some were not. I had memories that seem to conflict and I was smart enough to know that I could have been losing it. But the day came when I realized that it wasn't me, I realized that the conflict was being designed by the Monarchy. That was when I decided to destroy it." He paused as if recollecting a particularly painful memory and then continued, "I couldn't stand the actual day to day life there. The citizens were so banal, so tired. They made me tired to watch them. It was as if they were waiting to die, as if the chore of moving about frustrated them but they were too insolent and bitter to end it all. I wanted to end it for them, for me as well. I wanted them to be happy and dead, so I could be happy and alive and away from all of 'em. Ahhh...wishful thinking, I guess. There wasn't going to be such an easy solution and I knew it. I thought to myself, 'You are going to have to be creative to find your way out of this one, you are going to have to outdo yourself this time.' I began to do research on the Monarchy and the history of the Judicial Rising. It didn't take me long to understand what they were doing."

"So you collected data in order to develop ways to stop them?" asked Sigil.

"More than that," Engineer answered. "I actively built systems, both physical and conceptual, that worked directly against their plan. I had software scouring databases to revive old languages, picking out old words from standard Judicial English and cross-referencing them, I had holo VR systems running guerrilla ads on the streets, displaying counter-arguments against their main slogans. But in the end, it wasn't enough. In the end, all we had was the Crax. It's the only place left, where they don't control everything. If I hadn't found the Label, I think I would have lost hope by now."

Sigil nodded and the conversation went on, but, seated in the back seat, Anomalie had stopped listening. She stared out the window at the darkened streets and thought about Mara, where she might be, and the consequences of losing her.

THEY WERE APPROACHING the position that Tobi's trail had led them to when Engineer slowed the car, finally stopping it some distance away; all three stepped out of the car at the same time and turned to face the objective. There was a set of concentric rings made up of different sized tents, surrounded by a fenceline of heavy barbed wire. The larger tents seemed to be concentrated near the center, with the smallest, perhaps only large enough for two soldiers to sleep in, scattered near the outer edge. The entire collection was set into a basin cut into the ground, likely a large crater from a heavy bomb detonation during the Culture War, and bracketed on three sides by the rubble of broken buildings and torn pavement. On the fourth side, there was a tall hill rising above and to the rear of the encampment. Inside the ring of wire, Legionnaires moved to and fro, in a seeming state of preparation. On two sides of the ring, there were gates cut into the fence, and each gate was manned by two guards.

Just outside the fence, the light dropped off sharply; in the patchy shadows, lights could be seen moving about, carried by Crax children who had gathered near the gates to scavenge for food or trash that might be left behind by the Legionnaires. Sigil took charge and outlined the plan.

"We will have to hit hard and hit fast. Because this is a Judicial encampment, there will be three hundred and sixty degree security. Also, they are expecting us. So, Anomalie, prepare to face heavier odds than the last time. Engineer, what tech do you have that can help us here?" He spoke quickly and crouched in the snow. He began to draw some figures with his finger, rapidly sketching a mock-up of the target.

"I have a small satellite link that will feed realtime information from the Label directly into Anomalie's implants. I can patch Tobi's signature into that so that she can find his location. I'm sorry that I can't get you closer to Mara but I don't have a way to track her anchor's location," said Engineer, pulling the link from his satchel to show them. "I also have a jamming device that should be able to break up local Judicial communications. I'm afraid to use it in case it also affects Anomalie. I should only use it as a last resort."

"Very well. Assuming that the target is a basic circle, we can outline our assault as such..." He poked his fingers into the snow, designating marks for himself, Engineer and Anomalie, outside the ring of the enemy position. "Anomalie, since you will be fed Tobi's location, you are going to be the main assault element." She nodded as she crouched down next to him. "Do you see that higher area on the far side of the target?" He pointed to where a hill rose gently away on the opposite side of the lights.

"I see it," she replied.

"Good. That's *here* on this terrain model." He dragged his finger across the snow. "I'm going to that position with Engineer. They've made a slight mistake by not taking the higher ground, but I'm assuming that they wanted the natural cover that this depression provides them. We have to be there so that we can observe your movement and so that Engineer's jamming signal won't be blocked by concrete, should we be forced to use it."

"Got it," she chirped.

"The two of us will leave our present position first and will signal you through the satellite link once we're in position on the far side. *You* will approach, using stealth, as closely as you can from *this* direction. This places me in a position to attack across your line of movement, without hitting you, until you reach the center of the circle, understand?"

She nodded again. She was beginning to feel her heart beating faster.

"Do not, I repeat, *do not* use the Archon until it is completely necessary. We want to get as close to Mara as possible without the enemy being aware that we are on the objective. Every second counts. Once we activate the Archons, every gun down there will know where we are. Got it?" he said.

"Got it," she repeated.

"First, go for Tobi. Find him and force him to bring you to Mara if he knows where she is. If he can't or won't tell you within one minute, then we assume that her location is somewhere near the center of the defenses. As soon as you have trouble, activate the Archon. I will do the same, and we will both push toward the center until we find her."

He stood, and scraped his boot across the sketch.

"Okay. It is a simple plan, and dangerous. Both for us and for Mara." He took a breath and let it out. "But we are pressed for time so it should suffice. After we have her, we return back to this position to use the car for escape. Is everybody ready?" Engineer and Anomalie nodded in unison, then Sigil beckoned to Engineer and they both trotted off, taking a curving route to the peak of the hill, leaving Anomalie standing alone.

She began walking softly through the snow, toward a small berm that she could crouch behind, while still keeping the peak in sight. From there, she could see the entire face of the encampment with the peak of the hill directly to the right and above it. Through the hazy fog, she could see small swinging lights that moved in front of the Judicial command post. In the dead man's zone, between where she lay and the wire, she saw the silhouettes of children scurrying past.

She focused and zoomed the visual on her HUD, catching a tight image of one group. She had seen this before, children on the streets at night, abandoned. They seemed to make a game of it and they had the same little cliques and teams that the wealthy kids had. They frolicked beneath the dim streetlights, never hearing the call to dinner. Dinner never came. There was just the nagging tug from inside their bellies that cast a slight tarnish on their glow. Children always smiled while they played but there was an edge to the smiles of these children. They were playing... and they were hunting as well.

This was a Crax gang. Too/Sicks Crew, Tobi's bunch. She realized it as she sharpened the focus on her visual. They had similar quilted coats and spiked out hair. She saw kids as young as five or six years old and her stomach turned. She wouldn't be able to attack them, she wasn't even going to think about doing something like that. She hated the Judicial Monarchy, the system that she'd been forced to live under for her whole life. She hated the Judicials, she had seen too many people around her abused by them to feel sympathy for the Legionnaires. But poor kids? Abandoned kids? She identified with them. She understood all too well what it was like to not belong, she'd fantasized about joining a gang. If she'd had the chance, she would have been right there with them. She was furious at Tobi for taking Mara, and she knew that the gang probably had something to do with it, but she immediately decided that she wouldn't attack a child. She was going to have to figure out a way around them.

She began to shift from her hiding spot, carefully moving to the right, away from the gang. She was afraid that she would get too close to Sigil's line of attack but she was having trouble orienting herself with the sketch that he had drawn. It had looked simple on the terrain model but now, with the obstacles in the street and the shadows from the lights, she couldn't really tell how far to the right she had drifted. Then, she saw it. A path to the fenceline that would keep her out of sight of the gang. Angling even further to the right, there was a series of concrete pillars that had been part of an old collapsed overpass. They were almost totally demolished, with the tallest only being about three meters tall, but she saw that she could dart from one to the other without being exposed. If she was lucky, she would be nearly to the fence before she had to come out into the open.

She took a moment to think. If she began her approach now, she would be closer when she received the signal from Engineer. But if she was discovered before she received the signal, then she would spring the assault before Sigil was in position. She suspected that he had given her the lead on the attack because he was still weak from Tobi's attack at the lab, but didn't want her to worry about him. Now, looking ahead of her at the long distance from where she stood to the next shadow, she fervently wished that he was down here instead, and that she was up on the hill, looking down. What was he thinking, sending her into the camp first? *He* was the soldier. He was an angel. She was only a teenage girl. She caught herself abruptly before she nerved herself out. She remembered what Engineer had said to her in the testing room. She wasn't just a teenage girl. She wasn't broken. There was something special about her blood, about her. And Mara needed her now. Colleen still needed her. She couldn't die here. She wouldn't. Her heart was pounding, she saw her monitor peaking into the red and she decided not to wait.

"Nobody's a nobody," she whispered to herself and went. She darted out from where she'd been hiding and ran, crouching low to the ground. She nearly toppled over when her toe caught against a high spot on the ground that was hidden in the shadows. The moving lights made it nearly impossible for her to see the terrain clearly but she made it to the first pillar, scraping her back along it until she came to the far edge. She quickly peeked her head around to where she had last seen the gang. She saw them, but they were making too much noise themselves to have heard her. She switched her HUD through various spectrums, searching for movement inside the fenceline but she only saw the two guards posted at the front gate. They stood slack, bored and fiddling with their weapons and gear.

She turned her head back to the path she had picked out and squinted, trying to see any obstructions that would trip her up again on her next sprint. Nothing was obvious so she took a final look at the gang to see if any of them were looking in her direction. When she saw their attention focused away, she went again. She pushed juice into her leg servos, and felt more speed kick in. This time, when she reached the pillar, she banged into it with a thump. She had misjudged the distance slightly in the shadows cast by the shifting lights. Hastily, she pulled herself around the corner and froze. She popped her head back around the corner and pulled it back. She hadn't seen anyone react to the noise but she wasn't sure. Where was the signal from Engineer? Why was it taking so long? Her heart was racing as she tried to control her breath. Whenever she used her servos on full, it took more energy from her body and she felt it in her lungs and heart. She glanced at her pulse in her HUD and saw it fully in the red now. She fought to quiet her breathing and slowly pulled herself along the concrete of the pillar. Only two more to go and she would be near the fence. She wasn't sure where she was in relation to the peak of the hill anymore. Everything looked different from how it had on the sketch. It was stretched out and twisted and she couldn't remember how the plan was supposed to go anymore. It was simple, Sigil had said. He had described it so quickly and confidently that she had been sure that it would work. But now, halfway between the safety of the dark and the danger of the fence, it seemed impossible. She badly wanted to go back, but she thought of Mara, trapped inside the encampment and she gritted her teeth. She remembered when she had been caught by troopers, when she was fourteen, and she felt rage. She pushed on.

She was about to bolt to the next pillar when she heard a voice.

"Oiisse! 's a chick by da pylon, neh!" A kid's shrill voice cut through the dark. Anomalie froze, her breath catching in her throat.

"Eh? What you seen?" came another, older voice.

"A chick. Ran behind da pylon," said the first voice, with rising excitement. Anomalie's mind raced. Without hesitating, she pushed herself forward and out from behind the pillar. When she faced toward the sound, she saw a tiny version of Tobi trotting toward her. The boy was about eight or nine, wrapped in a too-large, quilted coat, like the rest of them wore. He stopped short when he saw her standing in front of him, her feet set widely.

"Who you be, neh?" he exclaimed. "You in Too/Sicks yard now," he challenged, his face defiant. Behind him, Anomalie saw another, larger boy walking towards her. He was leading a number of boys and girls, and his face was angry. She felt herself being scanned by their 'plants.

"I'm Anomalie," she said, trying to smile. "I'm lost. I'm not from the Crax." Her brain was working furiously, her eyes went to the encampment. She saw one of the guards turn his head toward the disturbance, unsure of what was causing it.

"Where you from, neh?" snapped the older boy, still coming toward her. "Only Crax kids down here, sis. Only Too/Sicks kids in dis yard, believe it." He walked past the younger boy and pushed him to the rear. The other members of the crew began to drift to her sides and surround her, soft lights swinging from the gear that they held aloft.

"I'm looking for Tobi. From Too/Sicks," she attempted. "He knows my little sis." She backed up a step, but put her feet into a fighting stance, hoping they didn't notice in the dark.

"He not here, neh. He inside, with da Judies," said the older boy suspiciously. He stepped forward and pushed his hand against her chest, pressing the anchor into it. She stumbled backward but regained her footing. "You in da yard. That be bad, sis. So yo neh," he growled.

"So yo neh," repeated a few of the other kids, nodding. They began to come closer and Anomalie saw the guard at the gate motion to his partner, pointing in her direction.

At that moment, she heard a crackle in her implants. A static-filled voice filled her ears.

"Anomalie. This is Engineer. We've located Tobi. He's inside, near the center..."

She didn't wait to hear the rest. Her system flooded with fear and adrenaline and she felt her joint servos spin up. She reached out with her left hand and grabbed the collar of the taller boy, twisting her fingers into it. She pulled back her right shoulder and fist and her face pulled into a grimace of anger. She saw the boy's eyes widen, as her fist shot forward and smashed into the center of his face. She felt his jacket pull against her grip and she let go. He slumped to the ground. The smaller boy leaped forward but she jammed out her foot, the bottom of her shoe connecting solidly with his chest. The little boy flew back and sat down hard, all the breath squirting out of him. She spun toward the fenceline and started running, pushing a girl out of her way as the girl reached for her arm. Anomalie stripped her arm out of the grip and took off, zigzagging. She heard the reports of the guards rifles and heard projectiles whiz by in the night air. Her eyes scanned right and left along the fence, searching for data that could help her. Her HUD lit up as she scrolled through icons frantically. There was nothing that was going to help her get through the fence, it was built just to keep her out. As the fence loomed into view, she reached down to the stone around her neck and grasped it in her hand, squeezing tightly.

"Fuck it. This *is* trouble," she whispered to herself. She felt her HUD filling with the strange icons, labeled in Angelic script. She had the sense of another set of eyes peering out through the same display. Her system filled with energy as she felt the armor of the Archon form around her body. She kept on running and she felt bullets bang into her left side and helmet as the guards zeroed in on her sprinting form. The song that Sabaoth sang erupted in her head, crashing forward, wrathful and ecstatic. She reached the fence and dropped into a crouch, planting both feet together into the earth. She sprang, her body shooting upward and over the fence, slowly cartwheeling above the barbed wire. She landed facing the guards as they paced toward her, firing at her with a steady rate of fire. Her eyes burned, and she looked down at her fist to see the dark, blood red sword materialize in the air, crimson smoky droplets falling from the blade. She felt her voice rise in her throat and become a scream of fury. With two sharp, instantaneous motions, she both passed and cut the two sentries down, the blade slicing through their armor and rifles like a laser.

"Anomalie. Can you hear me?" The voice sounded in her ears, but she could barely hear it through the sound of Sabaoth's song. She turned toward the center of the camp and, with a burst of speed, bolted forward.

The alarm had immediately spread through the camp; Legionnaires were pouring out of their tents. They came swarming from the rear of the camp to the forward gate where Anomalie had breached. She saw a flash of bright light far in front of her and above as she saw Sigil activate Adonaios in the distance. She saw their golden shape rise from the hill and take off like a rocket, leaving a comet-like tail behind it. Then, she saw a real rocket, being loaded into a rocket launcher by a two-man crew and aiming directly at her. The rocket crew had run into the lane between the tents and got their position quickly; Anomalie had barely an instant to react. In her HUD, she saw Angelic script scrolling faster than she could follow and she saw the cross-hair glimmer into the center of her vision. There was a loud blast and a cloud of smoke from the rocket crew. She felt a strong tug from the anchor and the armor jerked to the left, neatly sidestepping the warhead as it roared past. The rocket went into the wire behind her but didn't detonate there, it slid through and struck one of the concrete pillars that she had used for cover on her approach. She didn't look back as it exploded, shattering the pillar into a thousand shards of rock. Instead, she focused the cross-hairs on the dissipating plume of smoke that hid the rocket crew. She sped forward, kicking up a burst of snowy mud behind her. The sword flashed twice and she was through them, still picking up speed.

There were more Legionnaires massing ahead of her, but she ignored them. She was trying to get her bearings amid the tents; she veered around a corner, feeling the armor send a massive jolt of power into her joints. Her legs churned against the ground and she felt her feet gain traction. She shot down the lane between the tents as she headed for the center of the camp, feeling bullets banging into the armor as she ran.

She heard the voice in her ears again. "Anomalie. I see you." It was Engineer's voice. She heard it more clearly now, although the clash of Sabaoth's song was still ringing inside her head. "I'm sending Tobi's position to your HUD. Stand by." An instant later, she saw a glowing blip appear in her HUD, just to the right of the cross-hairs. She took the next corner and the blip moved to the center of the sights. There was a tent ahead of her, at the far end of the lane.

She covered the distance in seconds and skidded her boots against the icy ground. She twisted, trying to regain control but she was moving too fast. She burst through the flaps of the tent like a cannonball, shoulder first, and crashed, rolling across the floor of the tent. Her gyros spun and she was back on her feet instantly, scanning side to side, searching for Tobi or Mara. She saw him, seated in a chair to the side of the tent but he was not alone. Standing next to him was another figure, clad in green armor that glowed at the joints with threads of pale green luminescence.

She rushed towards Tobi, shouting. "Where is she, you little—?" But, before she could reach him, the armored figure stepped forward and stood between them. Anomalie didn't stop. She leaped forward, her arm bringing the sword down in a vicious slash. The armored figure made a slight movement and swatted her aside with both arms, dodging the sword easily. She smashed into the ground, stunned. It lowered itself, cat-like, into a crouching position and sprung after her.

It leaned forward above her and showered her with its fists. The figure's armor plated knuckles pounded into her like a jack-hammer from her helmet to her thighs. Anomalie could feel the sharp impacts through her armor, painful chisel points in her skull, ribs and legs. Then, the figure straightened and with a powerful kick, catapulted her through the wall of the tent. The heavy tent fabric tore open and Anomalie landed roughly on the ice outside. She rolled again and again and tried to swivel to her feet but, before she could raise herself up, another kick sent her sprawling. The visual display of her HUD was nothing but digital noise, and her gyros couldn't keep up with the spinning image in her eyes. She sucked in a large breath, shaking her head in an attempt to clear her view. In between the flickering icons, she could see the armored figure stalking toward her.

The figure closed the distance in a flash and Anomalie tried to swing her sword to cut it down but the sword was fading in and out of existence. When her arm came around to the front, the blade vanished totally and Anomalie's fist passed uselessly by the figure's face. She twisted awkwardly to her left and the figure reached out and grasped her body roughly with both hands. It lifted her into the air, swung its hips beyond her and threw her down. Her legs swung up, pinwheeling above her, and she crashed to the frozen ground again.

A golden flash impacted the pale green figure with an explosion of light. Dazed, Anomalie picked her head up slowly, blinking away the afterimage. Sigil was standing where her attacker had been a moment before, the gold-colored plates of his armor giving off wisps of faint smoke. She looked to the left and saw her opponent on the ground, at the end of a deep furrow in the earth. It began to rise to its feet, and Sigil snapped over his shoulder to her.

"Go back and get Tobi. I will deal with this one." He turned to the green armor and raised his hands into a fighting stance. "There may be others in the camp. Be vigilant."

She gingerly pushed herself to her feet, wincing as streaks of pain shot from her injuries. "Who the hell is that?" she muttered, wobbling slightly as she straightened up. "Another Archon?"

"Yes. Another Archon," he said. The green Archon's wearer started to circle warily, eyeing Sigil for an opening. "Hurry, Anomalie. It will not give you another chance. Get Mara."

She nodded and ran to the opening in the tent, ignoring the green Archon as it followed her with its eyes. As she reentered the tent, she heard the clash of the two Archons behind her as they began their contest. She strode to where Tobi was still cowering in the chair and, grabbing his jacket, she lifted him out of the chair and held him fast. He tried to pull away but she shook him violently so that his teeth clattered. He went limp and stared fearfully at her.

"Glad you're still here. I thought I would have to run you down," she said coldly.   "That wouldn't have been pretty. Where is she, Tobi?" She gave him another shake to drive home her mood. He swallowed, nearly choking on his panic.

"She wid another monster, neh. Like you, and da green one. Mech monster," he spluttered.

"Where?" she shouted, pulling him closer to her face. He was nearly hyperventilating, sucking in his breath in gasps. He tried to choke out some words, but couldn't. She nearly threw him away in frustration but thought better of it. "Fine. Show me," she ordered. He nodded frantically and she dragged him stumbling back through the shredded wall of the tent. Sigil and the other Archon were nowhere to be seen but the signs of their battle remained on the ground outside. Some of the tents were burning and the bodies of Legionnaires were strewn around. She hauled Tobi out in front of her and turned his face to look directly at her.

"Where did you see her last? Just point," she commanded. He held his arm out to the side, pointing at a tent, larger than the others, one row away. She squinted through the smoke in the direction that he pointed, and nodded. "Ok. You're coming with me," she said.

"No, no, no! I not goin' in there, neh! They tear me up, believe it!" protested Tobi weakly. Anomalie ignored him and loaded her servos. She felt the heat in her legs as they charged. Then, dragging Tobi behind her, she sprinted to Mara and whatever monster had stolen her.

She slowed when she came to the front of the tent and scanned it. There were people inside, but she couldn't detect any signals being emitted. That meant that they were un-wired, like Sigil and Mara. She dropped Tobi unceremoni-ously and moved cautiously. Unwired people made her ner-vous; it was unfathomable to her how Sigil and Mara could function without implants. She couldn't be sure, but there appeared to be only two signatures inside the tent. She motioned to Tobi to be silent, and looked around the camp. It was nearly abandoned, the few remaining opposition were either wounded or had realized that their weapons were impotent against the Archon armor. She didn't see Sigil or the green Archon, so she crept slowly to the flap of the tent and prepared to enter.

"There's no need to hide out there. You won't be taking her from us," a voice rose softly from inside the tent. Anomalie lifted the tent flap and looked past it. Inside, she saw Mara sitting calmly on a chair in the center of the tent; beside her she saw a young man in black Judicial armor. She entered, a look of barely controlled fury on her face.

"Who are you?" she asked. She could see that Mara knew him. The little girl wasn't restrained in any way. She didn't look afraid or worried. She didn't run into Anomalie's arms. Instead, she looked upward at the man with a happy smile on her face. Anomalie moved forward slowly, "Hi Mara. Come to me…We've come to get you and take you someplace safe." She glanced at the man. He stood casually, with his hand resting on Mara's shoulder, not reacting to Anomalie's movement at all. Anomalie sensed something awful from him, some power that she couldn't pin down. The armor that he wore was standard issue for Judicial officers. She had seen it dozens, if not hundreds, of times before. But, she couldn't escape the feeling that he was even more powerful than she, even with Sabaoth.

"I'm her brother," the man said flatly. "And she belongs with her family." He still hadn't moved anything other than his mouth when he'd spoken. Anomalie looked in his eyes and saw a cold bitterness. There was a barely covered anger that was just below the surface of his expression, but it was not like the anger that fueled Sabaoth or herself. Theirs was a hot, muscle-clenching anger that reveled in movement and freedom, the anger that a wild horse showed when someone tried to break it to the saddle. This man's anger was cold and still and dead, so dead that it was nearly impossible to detect. It was anger with no cause or reason. Anomalie realized suddenly that it was the anger of cruelty and torture. She knew then that she would never leave Mara alone with this man again.

"Maybe she is..." she answered in a slow, measured tone. "Maybe she's not..." She inched her boot forward slightly, trying to gauge her options. Still, he didn't react. He just stood there, motionless except for his eyes that seemed to drink in what she was thinking. She saw that he was not afraid of her at all. That he knew that she had destroyed a battalion of Judicial armor and had fought her way past his guards to stand here before him. And even knowing that, he was supremely confident that she would not be able to take Mara from him. "But she should still come with me. We can figure out who's who or whatever later." She was stalling for time, trying to work out a plan that didn't end in either her or Mara getting hurt or killed. She was afraid to move or to do anything at all; she didn't want to push Mara's brother to some extreme act. She slowly reached her hand out to Mara, palm up. "Please Mara, come to me." She beckoned gently with her fingers. "Let's go find Sigil."

At the mention of Sigil's name, Solomon's eyes narrowed. He lifted his hand from Mara's shoulder and with a small, deft motion, traced an Angelic character in the air. Anomalie saw it float and then drip away only an instant before a crushing force struck her.

"Sigil. Again with Sigil," he said, still softly, but with a hard edge. "My father told me the truth about *him*." Anomalie felt her armor grow hot, and felt a pressure come at her from all sides. It was as though she was held in a huge vise, squeezing her bones into her guts. She felt her neck contort painfully and her shoulders and ribs move inward. The armor's joints became orange, then yellow and then white hot. She fell to her knees. Mara slid from the chair and looked at Solomon with an angry glare.

"Solomon! Stop it! She's my friend, Namie." She waved her hand as if batting away a fly and the pressure around Anomalie lessened immediately. She fell forward onto her face in the mud, gasping for breath. Solomon spun toward Mara and grasped her shoulders, lifting her back into the chair.

"Be quiet, Mara. I'm taking you to father." He looked back at where Anomalie lay and addressed her scornfully. "You would be wise to stay where you are. My sister is strong. I've always known that. But that armor and those anchors that you both wear are not toys to be played with. The Archons are stronger than she is; stronger than you could ever imagine. I've trained with the anchors for years while we searched for her, she can't stop me now." He reached to where the plates of armor met at the center of his chest and pulled an anchor from beneath it. The stone hung from its chain, swinging below his fist. With his other hand he wrapped his fingers around it.

Anomalie's mind raced as she pushed herself slowly to her knees. Her eyes flicked rapidly across the icons that floated in her vision as she searched for anything that she could use to her advantage. She rummaged through files and applications that she had squirreled away in her memory, opening and discarding them with increasing speed. In the background she heard the music of Sabaoth but she tuned it out, seeking a file that was at the very edge of her memory. As she staggered to her feet, she found it. There was a martial arts program that she had run by herself when she was alone in the Old Zone. *Yang Style Tai Chi Chuan.*

She had been bored by herself and had been watching old Chinese wuxia films from before the Culture War. She had loved the stories, tales of heroic swordsmen and women who went to the mountains of China to develop their skills. Then, they returned to use their strength to defend the weak and oppressed. Their movements had seemed so beautiful and powerful to her. She had run the program into her joint servos and let them guide her, but she had always had the sense that the movements had come from somewhere else, as if her arms and legs had anticipated the pressure from her joints.

As she lifted her head to face Solomon, she loaded the app and let the software guide her joints into a flowing stance. Her hands opened up like the petals of a blossoming flower, one behind and above her shoulder, the other stretched out toward Solomon. Then, she switched the software to the free fighting setting. She felt the anchor tug, and felt the now familiar pull on her arm as the sword shaped itself above her. As she watched Solomon squeeze the anchor in his fist, she heard Sabaoth's voice rise from the music. "In battle, fear is the guiding light," it said, still merged with the song. "Run to it, away from the darkness of cowardice. Be strong, girl." She nodded and gestured to Solomon, beckoning to him. "Come on then," she said.

Solomon smiled and dropped the anchor. It swung loosely around his neck. An instant later, light began to coalesce around his hands as he held them out to his sides. From each hand materialized a long, ornate axe, with symbols of Angelic script spiraling up the thick handles. The blades were double edged and seemed to be formed of a shining black shadow. He twisted his wrists and the edges swallowed the light in the tent. Mara tried to slide from the chair again, but he reached out and pushed her into the seat with the back of his hand. "I'm stronger than you now, Mara. I knew that I would be. Stay here."

He lifted the axes as if testing their weight and then shifted himself to the side slightly, holding both axes in front of him. Then, he struck. He covered the gap between them with one sliding step, crossing his legs and crouching and then exploding forward. The axes struck around her, a swirling blur as they cracked off the flat of her sword. Her boots carved a series of curves in the dirt as she twisted and lowered her hips. Her arms and shoulders rotated and spun, the sword meeting each blow squarely. In her HUD, she could see the kung fu software spitting out encouragement and scores as her processors churned to keep up with the incredible speed of the movements. After a moment, the program glitched and gave up monitoring the free fighting. She poured more juice into her joints but Solomon's last attack connected. His blade crashed into the armor on her shoulder and pushed her back. Her boots dug deep furrows into the mud and she slid to a halt. The kung fu program whirred through some arithmetic and announced *HIGH SCORE!!*. She took a deep breath, faced Solomon and moved to the attack. In her HUD, there was a tiny animated icon of an old bearded Chinese man, jumping up and down, celebrating.

She swung the sword loosely in her hand, swiveling her wrist a few times before finally surging forward. The kung fu software instantly computed the best probable combination of strikes and defenses. The servo assists in her joints silently adjusted, receiving data from her gyros and her eye implants. The data combined and her sword flashed through a lighting fast series of attacks. Solomon shifted his weight and his axes intercepted each slashing cut. His last block hooked the blade of Anomalie's sword, and he pulled her forward with a savage tug, his legs widely spread in a sideways horse stance. Anomalie's system couldn't keep up. She felt her gyros shift as they failed to manage her balance. As she stumbled past Solomon, he struck the back of her helmet with his elbow. She saw a white flash of light as the immense power of the blow rang through the helmet. Once again, she fell to her elbows in the mud, stunned and disoriented.

"You can't beat me, little grid girl," said Solomon as he turned to stand above her. "Even with an Archon helping you, you could never win. And now you'll die because you tried." He lifted his axes high above his head and prepared to swing them down to the crease of her neck.

There was a terrific noise and flash of light as he was struck in the center of his chest by Sigil's spear. It protruded through the wall of the tent and pushed Solomon back. His axes missed their chosen mark, but one of his blades hurtled down with terrible force. It struck Anomalie just below her knee and cut through armor, muscle and bone. She didn't scream. Sigil slashed through the wall of the tent with the return swing of the spear and stepped inside to stand between Solomon and Anomalie's prone body.

Anomalie could now see blurry, pixelated images in her HUD. Her maintenance cycle was starting again; her system had crashed. Dizzy and nauseous, she tried to crawl away from Solomon and toward where Mara still sat on the chair. Her heart was palpitating dangerously; her sensors were showing critical emergency readings and she could feel vomit rising from her guts. She blinked rapidly, trying to focus on Mara as she dragged herself forward through the mud.

Sigil strode toward Solomon and prepared to thrust his spear. But Solomon was too quick. One of his axes vanished and he traced a symbol rapidly in the air and Sigil's blade was caught in a web of glimmering netting. Sigil twisted the shaft of the spear and pulled it back but the netting would not give way. Solomon spun to his knees and yanked the netting, pulling the spear from Sigil's grasp. It spun toward the wall of the tent behind Solomon and tore through, land-ing in the snow outside. Anomalie could not pull herself forward any further. Through the digital haze in her vision, she saw Solomon stand, trace another symbol and move his hands in a flowing motion. He settled back into a cat stance and pushed his hands forward slowly. She saw Sigil lower his helmet, a mask of glaring ferocity, and walk directly to-ward the floating symbol. He tried to push through it but the symbol expanded and then contracted tightly around him. Solomon clenched his fist and the laces of light that wrapped around Sigil shrunk.

Solomon turned toward Anomalie and laughed, a look of hatred on his face. "Did they tell you that they're immor-tal? That they couldn't die?" She was nearly unconscious, she knew that she was going to die. She ignored Solomon and inched toward Mara. Her system could not reboot, it was starting to shut down, icons blinking off one by one. Sigil struggled against the snare that held him, but Solomon looked past him and spoke to Anomalie, looking into her eyes. "They taught me that they were beings of light. From the heavens. And that they lived forever." He raised both of his axes above his head and held them still. "But they *can* die. . ." His voice became even colder. "I'll show you how to kill an angel." He brought the axes down savagely, into the sides of Sigil's neck. At last, Anomalie screamed. Sigil's body crumpled into the mud, streams of blood spray-ing from his neck. Through tear filled eyes, she looked up at Solomon as he stood above where Sigil had fallen.

"You mother-fucker! I'll fucking kill you!" she screamed. Sabaoth's voice mirrored her's inside her head like a chorus. She looked back to Mara and she saw two arms in quilted sleeves wrap around her and pull her back toward the hole in the tent. Then, she felt herself being pulled out and away from Solomon. Her eyes rolled upward and she saw Engi-neer's gray beard above her and heard his heavy breaths as he hauled her backward. She struggled against him, trying to get back to her feet and back to Solomon.

"Anomalie!" shouted Engineer. "No! You can't. Just hold on, you're hurt terribly. Tobi has Mara." Her eyes rolled down and she saw her heel dragging a line in the mud and beyond it, Solomon emerging from the hole in the tent.

"Let me go!" she cried, sobbing uncontrollably. "Please..." Her tears were hot on her face as she stared fiercely into Solomon's eyes.

Just beyond her hearing she heard Tobi's voice. "Engineer, yo neh. Do it now. I got da kid. Hit it now!"

She twisted her head to the left with the last bit of her strength. She saw Tobi huddled over Mara, and Engineer's hand drop down onto a switch on a piece of equipment that she had seen him take from his lab. She heard a squelching radio transmission emit from the box.

– LABEL – DIRECTIVE –

– TEMPORAL MERGE INITIATED –

And she heard Solomon howl with rage as her vision faded to black.

Chapter 14

Inheritance

*Of Thomas' anger
and of Solomon's response*

THOMAS Worth cast a cold glare over Solomon. The youth felt his father's eyes boring into him but he didn't look up. They stood alone on the roof of the Judicial Palace.

"You failed for the second time, boy." Thomas' words were hard-edged and brutal. Solomon sensed the rising violence in the tone; he steeled himself and kept his face turned away. "Look at me when I speak to you!"

At the shout, Solomon looked up. Thomas did not conceal his anger; his face was that of a dignified, older statesman but Solomon knew better. Behind his father's eyes was something primal and savage, a seething inhuman fury. He gazed coldly at the creature that stared at him from within his father's face and set his jaw.

"Yes, I failed," he replied. "I'll not make an excuse for it. I'll simply find them."

"Not make an excuse?" returned Thomas. "Perhaps you should. At least make an attempt to explain away your incompetence. You are a child of a Lord. A supreme commander of the Angelic host. How do you explain losing a third-rate, mercenary angel, and a teenage girl?" Thomas clenched his fists and leaned toward his son. "And you were accompanied by Archons yourself. Pathetic," he spat.

Solomon bristled but stood resolutely. "Engineer was there and used some device. It distorted the local Akashic field and created some sort of tunnel or doorway. They stepped through before I could reach them. But I didn't lose the mercenary, Sigil is dead." He stared defiantly at his father but Thomas had turned away to look over the stacked towers of the grids.

"Dead? Then where is his body?" Thomas lifted his arm and gestured across the ferro-crete landscape of the grids. "Did it vanish like a ghost in the machine?" He snorted. "Do you realize the gift I've given you? You were not meant to live. You were only born in order to create your sister. There were to be two, according to the contract that I sealed. Two children, one vessel. You could have been destroyed and my plans would still have born fruit." He shook his head. "Yet you were spared and trained along with your sister. Such foolishness. Such absurdity." He drew in a slow, deep breath. "It was your mother's doing. Behaving like the garbage that she was."

Solomon winced when he heard his mother mentioned but he held his tongue. He began to step toward his father but held back his footfall. Instead, he began to weave small signs in the air with his right hand held near his waist. His father turned back to face him.

"Well?" he started, "What is your excuse?" He was about to say more when he realized what Solomon was doing. He began to lift his hand but he was too late. Solomon completed writing the sign in the air and bolted toward his father, a glow of energy trailing from his right hand. He whipped his hand forward just as he reached his father and the edge of the roof, his hand connecting with the older man's chest. Immediately, the glow of energy spread from his hand to envelop Thomas, folding around him, encasing him, and feeding back into Solomon's clenched fist. Solomon was shaking with the strain; he bent at the knees and lowered himself to ground his body to the building. Thomas resisted, but Solomon screwed his heels into the roof. He pinched his eyes shut and let out a hard, hissing breath. A huge crack spread on the roof beneath his feet as his father struggled against the spell and the energy was directed through Solomon and into the Palace roof. The crack raced to the other side of the roof and blew a large chunk of stone from a corner tower. Solomon grunted with exertion and opened his eyes to stare into his father's face. He smiled cruelly as the energy changed from yellow to white and his father began to burn inside the halo of light.

"He did not vanish like a ghost, father. He died like an Angel. Like a demon." His voice was low and taut as he struggled with the massive flow of energy rushing through him, but he held. He raised his hand and Thomas Worth lifted into the air above the edge of the Palace, his skin sizzling and popping as he looked through the haze of heat at

Solomon. "Like you will now, father. And Mara too when I find her. You lie father, or you have been lied to." He opened his fist and his father's body drifted slowly away from the edge of the roof and hung above the grid hundreds of feet below. "This I know. There is no such thing as a being of light." Solomon swung down his hand and his father burst into flame and hurtled downward toward the grid. Solomon didn't look over the edge to see his father fall; he knew that there would be nothing but ash and a few bones remaining when his body struck the earth. He straightened and breathed in and wiped the perspiration from his eyes. Then, without looking back, he turned and walked into the Palace.

Chapter 15

Dark Days

---

*Of Solomon Worth
and of the pain of the World*

WHAT are the little noises, the tiny tugs? The almost invisible itches that begged to be scratched before you can think clearly. She tried to push them to the rear, back behind the scenes of her conscious mind but they were still there. There was a feeling of hunger that would not be satiated. There were memories of a time when there was more than enough to eat and she whispered in her dream about those times, the way wealthier children would speak about a favorite movie or a visit from a favored uncle. She whispered about meals that she had shared with her friends before the hunger. More often than not, the memories were filled with embellishment and took on a sort of fantastical fairy-tale quality. They competed with each other and tried to better the dreams from before. Each tale was grander than the last, until finally, she whispered aloud, in a dry voice, "I'm hungry…"

The first things that Anomalie became aware of were the little noises, a creaking chair, plastic wheels being rolled across a hard floor, the rustle of clothes near her head. She tried to open her eyes, but the brightness pained her. "I want food…" she whispered again. This time, someone answered her.

"I'll get you something. But, you have to promise to take it slowly, you've been asleep for over a week." It was a woman's voice, gentle but firm. Anomalie heard the sounds of the woman rising from the creaky chair and then, her footsteps as she left the room. She tried again to open her eyes and this time, she could keep them open for longer. She slowly slid her pupils to the side of the bed and saw Mara sitting on the floor, playing with a toy truck, rolling it back and forth in a noisy curve.

"Mara…" she scratched out. Mara didn't seem to hear her. "Mara," she said again, clearer and louder. Mara looked up and, when she saw life in Anomalie's eyes, her face opened into a brilliant smile. She dropped the truck, jumped to her feet and ran to Anomalie's side.

"You're awake!" she cried happily, reaching across Anomalie's chest to hug her. Anomalie felt the weight of the anchor pressing into her beneath Mara's embrace. She looked down at Mara's hair below her chin and laughed dully.

"Uh-huh, I'm awake. Barely. Where are we?" she asked.

"This is my house!" Mara exclaimed, twisting her head to check Anomalie's response. "My old room is down the hall and Solomon's is on the other side. This is my mommy's room. You're in her bed," she finished, finally letting go of her embrace. She hopped back, away from the bedside, as the woman from before entered the bedroom, carrying a tray with a bowl and a glass on it. "That's my mommy," Mara said, pointing. Anomalie now saw the resemblance to Mara, the same dark, straight hair, the same deep, searching eyes. But Mara's mother didn't give off the otherworldly aura that Mara did, she seemed grounded and real. Dressed in casual jeans and a button-up collared shirt, she was the picture of normalcy. Anomalie couldn't make the connection between either of them and Solomon.

"Yes, I'm Mara's mother," the woman said. "It's nice to finally see you awake, Namie. But, Mara, Namie needs it to be quiet so she can get better." She helped Anomalie into a better position, rearranging the pillows behind her, and lowering the tray over Anomalie's lap. "So please, inside voice, okay?" she said, looking at Mara lovingly.

"Inside voice. Sorry..." answered Mara, hanging from the back of the chair.

"Mara, why don't you go outside and get Dr. Galen from the garage?" She looked down at Mara to catch her attention, "The doctor will want to know that Namie's awake."

"Okay, I'll get Engineer too," she said. She raced out of the room and down the hall, her footsteps diminishing quickly. Anomalie heard a door swing open and slam shut.

"So you're Mara's mom, huh?" said Anomalie slowly. She could weakly move her arms, so she tentatively lifted a spoonful of soup to her mouth and swallowed. She thought it was the most delicious mouthful of anything she had ever tasted. She had a few more and, in between swallows, spoke again, "Is she okay? Mara, I mean."

She thought of saying, *"Umm... I know this sounds loony, but what year is it? I'm not a Terminator or anything..."* but she refrained, she didn't know how real that vid was to these people.

"She's fine," said Mara's mother. "She bounces back very quickly. She always has. Except once," she added, with perhaps a slight touch of bitterness in her voice. "And you can call me Emily. Emily Worth. I'm pleased to meet you."

"Nice to meet you too, I'm Anomalie Harper." Emily held out a hand to her and Anomalie shook it limply. She was still numb from whatever they had given her to keep her asleep; she couldn't feel much from her chest down. She let her hand drop heavily to her side and leaned her head back against the pillow. Emily took the tray from her and set it on a small table in the corner. They heard the door swing open again, and this time a number of heavier footsteps sounded in the hall. The door to the bedroom opened again and Engineer burst into the room.

"Look at you!" he shouted. "I knew that they couldn't stop you!" He ran to the side of the bed opposite Mara's mother, ignoring her hand motions urging him to stay quiet. "You are definitely something special." He picked up her arm and began to inspect it closely. "Are you feeling any residual effects from the temporal shift? Any slurring in speech or kinks in your joints?" He peered at her face as though she was under a microscope. He looked so funny to her that she nearly couldn't hold back her laughter, but no sooner had a smile formed on her lips than she thought of Sigil and frowned. Another man had entered the room behind Engineer, following closely on his heels.

"Back up from her, Engineer," the stranger admonished, slapping Engineer's hand sharply, causing him to release Anomalie's arm. "Please give her some space. She's only just regained consciousness." Engineer scowled but moved back. The stranger inserted himself between Engineer and the bed and placed a physician's bag on the nightstand. "She's not a device for you to download data from, she's my patient. What's more, she's been seriously wounded and I need to examine her and ask her some questions." He cast a stern look at the others in the room and waved his head toward the door. Obediently, Engineer stood and went to the door. Mara's mother shooed Mara out after him and turned back to face Anomalie.

"Don't worry, he'll take good care of you. He's a good man." She smiled at him and said, "I'll be right outside if you need me, Michael." He nodded at her and waited until she closed the door softly behind her. Then, he focused his attention on Anomalie.

"Hello, Anomalie. I'm Dr. Galen. How are you feeling?" he said, in a kindly voice. He was young for a doctor, maybe in his thirties, and he wore khaki pants, a flannel shirt and glasses. He had a gentle look and manner but Anomalie still regarded him suspiciously. This doctor was from over one hundred years in her past, she had no idea what sort of primitive methods he might attempt to use on her. She reached down to the blanket that was spread over her and pulled it to her neck.

"Do you know about me?" she asked defensively, "What did Engineer tell you? I'm not like the patients that you're used to."

"Yes, Engineer explained as much as he could to me. I know that you're *augmented*. This is not entirely unheard of at this point in time, you know. Although we don't have the level of technology that has produced your implants, I can certainly treat your biological injuries. But, Anomalie, I have to discuss those injuries with you." He paused. "We've been able to keep you sedated while we worked on your ribs and head injuries, but I've had to deaden the nerves below your waist. Do you understand why?" He looked at her with compassion, but did not seem like he would wait long for her answer.

"I heard you say I was seriously wounded…" she began, searching in his face for a clue. "But I don't feel that bad. Only numb." She stopped, realizing that he was preparing her for something horrible.

Dr. Galen did not hesitate. He knew that it would only be worse for her if he was not as direct as possible. "Anomalie, your right leg was severed just below the knee." Her eyes went wide as the information took long seconds to sink in. Then, she threw the blanket away from her neck. Dr. Galen reached out and caught it with his hand, holding it close to her. "Take a moment and breathe, Anomalie. Just breathe calmly… That's it… just like that, breathe."

She tried to calm herself and follow the doctor's quiet voice. After a moment, she closed her eyes and tried not to think of anything. When she opened them, Dr. Galen was in the same place, waiting patiently for her.

"It's better if you do look at your wound today. But, if you're not ready, I can leave and we can do it together tomorrow. I can also give you something if you would just like to sleep some more this afternoon." He waited. She held her lips tightly together and looked away from him, staring at the wall. Then her eyes became determined and she looked at him directly.

"I want to see. Now, please," she said. He smiled and nodded. "Good. Engineer told me that you would say that. Let's take a look at how you're doing." He gently pulled the blanket down and away from her until she could see below her waist. She was wearing a hospital gown that tied in the back and, below the bottom hem, she saw her left leg, covered with purple bruises, on the bed. On the right side of the bed, she saw only a few inches of bandage, neatly wrapped and dotted with yellowish stains. She looked at it silently for long moments, thinking.

"I'd like to change the bandages, are you ready for that today, Anomalie?" Dr. Galen broke the silence softly. She nodded, with tears in her eyes and he rapidly removed the old bandage. After he inspected her leg, he took some fresh bandages from his bag and quickly applied them. When he finished, he looked at her.

"All finished. Other than being battered around, the rest of your system seems to be healthy. Your vitals are strong, and you are healing. I would like to keep a very close eye on you for these first few days that you're awake though. So, I'll be here in the house twenty-four seven should you need me." He stood, and turned to the door. "Should I send your friends in? They've been very worried about you."

She shook her head angrily and pulled the blanket tight around her neck. The doctor nodded as she threw her head against the pillow and turned her face away from him; he closed the door softly behind him.

Mycologie

At the edge of the forest,
a doorway is waiting,
nestled among the grass.
You cannot see it, or touch it, or lock it
and only the brazen may pass
Under the lintel and into the kingdom
where Pan and the Faerie rule
The key is not golden, nor silver, nor brass
but only a simple toadstool.

ENGINEER AND TOBI trudged upwards, along the mountainous path, far behind Mara's house. They had left the house early in the morning, before anyone else had awakened; Engineer had peeked in on Anomalie to see her sleeping soundly as they left. They had been hiking for nearly an hour.

It had been almost a week since Anomalie had regained consciousness but she still had not been strong enough to leave the bed. Engineer was becoming worried and had voiced his concerns to the doctor.

"She will be ready in good time Engineer," the doctor had replied. "When she feels ready, she will do it. She's very strong."

Engineer had nodded sullenly and stayed silent, he felt responsible for Tobi and it had ultimately been Tobi's fault that Anomalie had been injured and that Sigil had been killed. Now, he paused on the wooded trail and looked behind him to where Tobi was struggling upwards to him.

"Hurry up. I want to be back before noon," he called out, but Tobi didn't answer. Engineer watched him as he awkwardly moved between the trees and bracken, his boots seeming to clip and catch on every branch and root.

"This's crazy Engineer," huffed Tobi when he finally caught up. "I never seen da trees and dirt like this, yo neh." He struggled to catch his breath, looking all around him nervously. "There like wild animals out here too, believe it. "'This ain't da Crax for sure, neh."

Engineer gave him a moment's rest and then, motioning him forward, pressed on up the hill. "No, it's not. But, it's beautiful don't you think?" he said.

"Guess so," said Tobi shortly, "but weird too." He nearly fell, tripping over a fallen log and catching himself on a low hanging branch. "Ahh, fail!" he shouted, looking critically at his scraped palm. "Where we goin' anyway? What you lookin' for out here?"

"Something very special," replied Engineer. "Something that we don't have in the Crax. Or in the grids for that matter. I'll know it when I see it." Then he fell silent. They continued on without speaking for some time.

Suddenly, Engineer stopped short and pointed off the trail. "There," he said.

Tobi looked to where Engineer was pointing. "Just grass, neh? What you pointing at?"

"Come, I'll show you," said Engineer, stepping off the trail and into the wide clearing that opened in the forest. Tobi followed him, stepping through the tall grass. Engineer studied the ground in front of him as he walked, searching for something. "See, Tobi, where the grass is cut shorter? It's been chewed down. This is what we want." Puzzled, Tobi nodded but said nothing. "Step carefully, we don't want to damage any," said Engineer softly.

"Damage what, neh?" said Tobi.

"This," replied Engineer, crouching. He bent forward and moved some of the broken grass blades aside. Underneath, attached to a small pile of loamy earth, was a patch of mushrooms clustered together. He carefully plucked a few and held them out to Tobi. "Look closely. Do you see these colors?" Tobi leaned in carefully. The mushrooms had light dusty brown caps, with soft, robin's egg blue stems. Engineer turned them over and showed the underside of the caps to Tobi. "See here, the gills? Look inside the gills." Tobi looked and saw what Engineer was pointing out. Inside the gills was a glistening, golden dust. It was incredibly reflective, seeming to give off its own light. Tobi attempted to scan it with his implants but got nothing but static haze.

"Keep forgetting 'bout my 'plants..." he said mournfully. "Like bein' blind and deaf."

"Get used to it," said Engineer, understanding. "We're stuck here for the time being. So, use the Label connection and whatever they have for wireless. I know that it's not much, but figure it out." He began loading the mushrooms into small plastic bags and placing them carefully into his satchel. "Don't try to crack the other sats. They'll notice. Help me find more 'shrooms. They'll be in the chewed down spots."

Tobi nodded and began searching through the grass. "Never spot me inside those sats, believe it," he muttered.

"Don't do it Tobi!" said Engineer sternly. "I mean it."

"So yo neh. Okay," said Tobi reluctantly. "Oiisse! I got some!" He held up a handful of mushrooms for Engineer to inspect. Engineer double checked them and, when he was satisfied, put them in his satchel with the others. They slowly moved through the clearing, canvassing from edge to edge, until Engineer announced that they had collected enough.

An hour later, they emerged from the woods behind the little gray house and began walking across the large back yard. Exhausted, Tobi had his eyes locked on the ground in front of him; his thighs and feet hurt in a way that was entirely new to him. He looked up sharply when he heard a cry of excitement from Engineer; standing on the far side of the yard, leaning on a wooden crutch, was Anomalie.

She was dressed in an ash gray sweatshirt and sweatpants; the right leg was neatly pinned up behind her knee. On her left foot was her remaining black Converse Chuck Taylor basketball shoe. Dr. Galen was on her opposite side, gently guiding her with a hand on her shoulder but she shook it off. She lurched forward at first, but after a few steps, she propelled herself forward with confidence. Engineer ran across the yard and wrapped his bear-like arms around her in a smothering hug.

"Ouch. My ribs still hurt," she said, her voice muffled by his shoulder.

"Oh. Of course. Sorry," said Engineer, releasing her. "I'm so glad to see you out here." He was about to say something else when he saw Anomalie looking past him to where Tobi stood, hanging back in the middle of the yard. Tobi tried to lift his eyes to meet hers, but cast them down again to his feet.

"Anomalie..." began Engineer.

"Don't," she interrupted, her face stony. "What's up, Tobi? What are you gonna say?" She pushed Engineer to the side, her strength surprising him. "What are you gonna say to me?" she said, her voice rising.

Tobi's face slowly rose from the ground. He lifted his hand and pushed his goggles up into his hair. When he saw the empty space next to the crutch where her leg had once been, his face screwed up and tears began to pour from his eyes. He blinked and looked away.

"I had to, neh. I so sorry 'Nomalie. They was gonna kill me and da whole crew, believe it." He tried to control his sobs, but they poured out from him and he choked on his words. "I so really sorry. I can't..." His voice fell away as he wept.

Anomalie looked away from him as well and spat in the grass. "Say sorry to Mara, not to me," she said in a hot voice. "And you can never say sorry to Sigil. You can't do that, can you?" He shook his head. Anomalie looked up at Engineer. "I don't know why he's here," she said.

Engineer put his hand on her shoulder and led her away, toward the garage behind the house. "Come with me. We can talk alone in here." He looked over his shoulder at Dr. Galen to see if he would protest but he nodded and watched as they walked slowly away, Anomalie hobbling heavily on her crutch, Engineer propping her up with his hand beneath her free arm. As they entered the garage, Tobi continued to stand forlornly in the center of the yard.

Inside the garage was an array of humming computers arranged in a complicated series of connections. Behind the stacks of dingy towers and racks was a spaghetti of cabling and wires, leading to larger conduits that ran along the floor. Next to two of the walls were benches that contained makeshift chemistry equipment. To Anomalie, it looked like something out of a prehistoric documentary.

"Where did you get all this stuff?" she said in amazement.

"Tobi has been taking trips to the city with Dr. Galen and Emily. He's quite an enterprising thief," answered Engineer as he pointed her to a stool next to one of the benches. She awkwardly arranged herself on the stool and leaned her crutch against the bench.

"Nice. A thief *and* a kidnapper. Rad friend you got there, Engineer," she said dryly.

"I know that you're angry, Anomalie," he said. "But he is truly sorry. And he meant it when he said that the Judicials were planning on killing his entire gang. He's only thirteen years old, Anomalie. Try to understand."

"I understand that he got Sigil killed," she snapped. "And got me crippled. And—"

"No, Anomalie, he didn't. He didn't do those things," Engineer cut in brusquely "*Solomon* did those things. The Monarchy did those things. That boy only did what he thought was right by his friends. The same as you did." He paused. "Did you know that Mara left on her own with him?" he asked, watching her face carefully.

"What?" she exclaimed, "What are you talking about? Why would she do that?"

"You saw her when she was with her brother, you know that he wasn't holding her there. She *wanted* to go to him." He rearranged himself to face her directly. "Tobi told me that when he fired the signal in my lab, it knocked Sigil out of action but Mara was unaffected. He didn't know what to do with her. She *told* him that her brother was nearby, in the Crax. She knew where Solomon was. And she told Tobi to take her to him. So he did. Try to see it from his perspective, Anomalie. What would *you* have done to protect your friends?"

"And you believe Tobi?" she asked forcefully, but she remembered Mara's face inside the tent. Mara had not tried to escape from Solomon. She knew that Engineer was right. She glumly released a pent-up breath.

Engineer saw her expression change from anger to frustration. "I know that he's telling the truth. I've had him hanging around my lab since he was six years old. He lies all the time, but I know when he does." He stood, pushing the stool back. "There are some odd things about that little girl."

Anomalie nodded, giving in. "I'll try to talk to Tobi. I promise."

Engineer smiled. "Thank you. But, I didn't bring you here to talk about Tobi. Or Mara. I want to talk to you about you,"

"What about me?" she asked.

"Well, we don't have the same level of tech here that we're used to working with but, thanks to Tobi's little foraging trips, we have hacked together a reasonable workspace here." He waved his arm around the garage. "I want to continue testing you. And Mara as well. I've explained everything that I know to Dr. Galen and Mara's mother. They've explained some things about Solomon and Mara's father to me. They've agreed to help us to carry on our fight. That is, if you're willing."

Anomalie stared at Engineer, then looked down at her thigh, jutting off the stool, terminating in a bunching, pinned stump. "How?" she asked, "We're in the olden days. I only have one leg. Sigil is dead. How are we supposed to fight?" She remembered Solomon as he swung his axes down on Sigil. She remembered how easily he had beaten her. He had beaten them both, with Mara standing right there. With power like that, how could they expect to win? She shook her head. "I don't think we can do it."

Engineer lowered himself to bring his face closer to Anomalie's. "Listen to me, Anomalie. I told you that you were special, didn't I?" She nodded, still looking away from him. "Look at me," he said. "Look at me," he said again, holding her chin and twisting her face toward him. "You *are* special. Very special. I promised you that I would fix you, and I will. But you have to promise me that you won't give up. Can you do that, Anomalie?"

She looked into his eyes for a long moment. She thought of Solomon, she wanted to crush him for what he had done to her. To Sigil. She nodded.

"I promise," she said in a soft voice. "I won't give up."

"Good. We still have Mara. And we still have two anchors. Best of all, we still have you. And of course, my brilliant brain. Between myself and the esteemed Dr. Galen, and this bin of prosthetic legs that Tobi stole for you, we should have you back on your feet in no time."

WHEN THEY FITTED HER with the prosthetic leg, Anomalie didn't bat an eye. She had been enduring implant procedures since she was an infant and was only shocked by the primitive tools that Doc Galen used on her. Her operating system was equipped with a surgery application that would deaden her nerves at the site of an implant, so she needed no anesthetic. The app would also allow her to view real time diagnostics in her HUD during the procedure so that she could assist by talking Engineer and Doc Galen through the surgery.

"How did we get here anyway?" she asked, as Doc Galen was preparing to cauterize some of her tissue. They were in the garage workshop that also doubled as a medical and biology lab.

"What do you mean? How did we arrive in the Gray Mundane?" replied Engineer. He stood next to Galen, his eyes intently focused on the screen of a circuitry testing scope that was wired to Anomalie's hip.

Anomalie blew a stray lock of hair from off of her eyebrow, shaking her head. "No, I mean how did we get to this house? Did we just, like, land here?" She shifted a bit but Doc Galen glanced sharply up at her. She stopped moving and he went back to his work.

The doctor answered her question before Engineer could. "Mara knew her phone number and called her mother when you all arrived in this era. Emily and I went to pick the four of you up." He shook his head. "You were unconscious because of shock and loss of blood; It was actually touch and go there for a while. Luckily, Mara had the presence of mind to remember her old number after 2 years away from home. You might not have survived if she hadn't"

He finished up with the sealing of her arteries and tying off of muscle fibers. He nodded to and traded places with

Engineer, who lifted up the prosthetic leg and placed it on the table beneath Anomalie's knee.

"I'm going to be connecting to some of your sensor arrays, Anomalie," he said. "I'll need you to tell me what you see in your visual." She nodded to him. "There will be a series of colored discs that appear, I want you to tell me what colors you see as I calibrate the sensor connections." She nodded again. He continued. "After that, I'm going to attach the ankle servo to your gyro output and feed it back, to make adjustments. Should take about an hour for the system to learn. Got it?" She sighed and leaned her head back on the table. Pretty standard, she thought to herself. She began to doze off as Engineer started the calibration.

SOLOMON HAD SPOKEN BRASHLY to his father about Sigil's body, but he was troubled by it. After he had stricken the angel down, he had instructed his men to remove the body to the Palace and they had. But, until now, he'd been unable to inspect it because of the Archon armor that encased it.

Solomon went deep into the subterranean levels of the Palace and entered a small room where the golden armor lay prone upon a steel table. He nodded to the staff in the room and to the guards at the door. The staff filed out and the guards closed the door behind them, leaving Solomon alone with Sigil's unmoving body. He leaned near the armor, peering closely at the seam where the helmet met the throat. The armor had been sliced widely open at the neck by Solomon's axes, he was sure of it. But the armor was now intact, unblemished, as though it was newly forged. He looked closer, searching for the stone that had been around Sigil's neck, suspended by a chain. He realized that his ax had most likely sliced through the chain and that the anchor was lost. He grimaced. The anchors were an important puzzle; it was curious how Sigil and his allies had obtained them. Solomon had hoped to have the stone analyzed, to pry its source from it.

Solomon felt around the mask and the helmet, and as he did, the helmet separated from the throat guard. It rolled to one side, revealing nothing but empty space within. He picked up the helmet, stepping back in shock, and then he hurled it to the floor in a rage. As the guards pushed open the door to find the cause of the outburst, he slammed it aside and stormed past them. He walked briskly down the hallway and entered another room, a laboratory staffed by a researcher and two technicians. They bowed hurriedly as he entered but he waved aside the salutations.

"Show me the leg." he said. "Now."

The lead researcher moved quickly to appease him, gesturing to his assistants to comply. "Of course, Your Honor. I am keeping it in one of the stasis lockers. It is a tightly controlled environment. We monitor it from here with—"

Solomon cut him off. "I don't care about the technical nature of its storage. I need to examine it immediately. And don't call me 'Your Honor'," he finished, a dangerous expression in his eyes.

"My apologies, Your— umm…sir," replied the researcher lamely. "I only thought that, with your father away, you would become the new High Judge." The lab assistants had returned from the stasis locker and put a bundle on one of the workbenches. The lead researcher glanced at Solomon, who nodded. He began to unwrap the bundle.

"I have no need for titles—" said Solomon, "or salutes. I have something better." He took his eyes away from the object on the bench and saw the confused expressions on the faces of the researchers. "Power." he explained plainly. He waved the researchers back and they stepped away from the bench, leaving him room to maneuver around what he was inspecting. It was Anomalie's leg, roughly severed just below the knee joint, still encased in a sleek boot of blood-red armor. He looked more closely at where his axes had cut and he saw that the armor was not actually pierced there. Although the flesh of the leg had been cut neatly and the tibia and fibula bones had been more brutally cracked, the boot itself had seemed to simply part where his axes had made contact. It was as though the armor had allowed the axes to pass through and then had reforged itself at the edge of the amputated limb. His brows furrowed and he looked closer. He could see that her bones were those of a typical grid citizen, laced with alloy and circuitry that would have led from her knee joint servo housing down to her ankle and foot. He looked up to the researchers. "Have you found anything unusual about this sample?" he questioned. "Why is the boot not removed?"

One of the technicians looked at the lead researcher, who gestured to him to speak. He swallowed and began timidly. "The boot could not be removed, Your Ho— sir. If you look more closely, you will see that there is no seam between the armor and the flesh of the leg. It seemed that the only way to remove it would have been to destroy part of the sample, so we opted to leave it intact."

Solomon nodded his approval absently and did as the assistant suggested. When he looked more closely, he saw that what the technician said was true. At the cut, he could see that it appeared as if the armor and flesh had fused. "Do you have a theory?" he asked the lead researcher, without looking away from the leg.

"We think that it may have something to do with how the blades of your axes interact with matter, or perhaps other Archon based material. We haven't seen the effect before, but there is still much that we don't understand about Archon technology." the lead researcher replied. Solomon nodded. "Also, sir, there is another odd effect," the researcher said tentatively.

"Go on," prompted Solomon.

The researcher pointed at the leg. "The sample is being kept in a stasis locker in order to impede decomposition. But we've seen no signs of decomposition at all. The leg seems as if it was freshly severed. Other than some slight blood clotting, which would occur if the leg was still attached, it appears as a totally fresh wound. Rather bizarre, sir."

Solomon's eyes lifted from the bench and drifted up the wall toward the ceiling of the lab, unfocused in thought. After a few short moments, they refocused and he aimed them toward the researchers again.

"Very well. Keep me immediately informed of any changes in the status of this project." The researchers nodded and bowed in obedience as Solomon walked from the lab, deep in concentration.

THE REAR HATCH of the troop transport lowered as the craft dropped slowly from the sky above the Crax. For days now, Judicial drilling teams had been opening up huge rifts in the

Barrens outside of the Grids. Appearing as deep sinkholes, they were large enough to allow squadrons of aircraft to descend into portions of the Crax.

As the craft was touching the ground, Solomon strode down the ramp and stood, surveying the commotion before him. Flanking him on either side were the wearer of the green Archon armor and another, much larger figure, its Archon armor a dull, matte indigo. All around him there was activity as Judicial troops organized vehicles, weapons and other supplies. Solomon studied the frenetic bustle for a moment and then he signaled to a passing captain and the Judicial officer came running. The captain stopped before the three figures and bowed, saluting as his head came up.

"Yes sir?" he said. Solomon turned his head to the left and the right. In the corners of his vision there were intermittent flickers of digital snow swirling to the ground.

"Can't you do something about this interference, Captain? I'm not impressed by Engineer's coding tricks."

The captain nodded. "Yes, sir. We've located and disabled a number of his generators. It's only a matter of time before we find them all."

Solomon frowned in impatience. "You don't have any more time, Captain." He turned to the green Archon and nodded, nearly imperceptibly. The eyes behind the green mask blinked and the Archon bowed. It looked toward its indigo counterpart and beckoned. Both Archons began to walk slowly away toward the center of the Crax. Then, they began to trot and then run. As the huge, indigo Archon picked up speed, the green Archon sprang into the air, bat-like wings forming behind its shoulder blades. Within moments, they were streaking into the heart of the Crax. Solomon turned his attention back to the officer. "Where is Colonel Blackwood? Is he still here at the staging area? I want you to bring him a message from me."

"Yes sir, I believe the Colonel has not deployed the armored scouts yet so he is still in the command tent."

"Tell him to forget the scouts. I will relay intelligence to him real time, from this craft. Tell him to begin the assaults now."

As Solomon spoke, the captain glanced nervously upward as more troop transports and assault craft came into sight overhead, passing into the interior of the Crax. "Yes sir," he responded. "But sir, I'm not sure if you're aware that we've not begun the evacuation. We are about to both drop warning leaflets and do announcements from rovers on the streets. I was personally in charge of the evacuation planning. It should only take until early morning to complete."

Solomon's eyes filled with a dreadful chill as he looked at the officer. "I did not order any evacuation," he said coldly.

The officer looked slightly surprised, but quickly regained control. "Yes sir. But it is standard procedure, when doing these large scale raids, to do preliminary evacuation protocols. You, of course, are aware that we can't be as precise as we would like to be when covering such a large area. I'm—" Solomon held up a hand, stopping the officer short.

"No evacuation. Bring my message to Colonel Blackwood and complete your own preparations. The assaults will begin immediately." He began to turn back up the ramp into the troop transport.

"But sir..." interjected the officer. "The Crax is inhabited largely by children. I'm sure you're aware of Judicial policy on—" He stopped short when Solomon turned to face him.

"There is a *new* policy, Captain. Now that my father is gone, *I* set Judicial policy. *I am* the Judicial system now. You will find that things will be much different. Much faster." He turned back up the ramp. "Bring the message. Stand by to begin the assaults."

"Yes sir. Very good sir," answered the captain. Behind him, as he ran to relay the message, the hatch of the troop transport closed and the craft lifted into the air and swung away toward the Crax, followed by many, many more exactly like it.

Harvest

The season of Harvest is closing away,
Warmth vacates us, and light becomes cold,
Frost separates each glistening, dying leaf,
On every limb, every tree. . .
Then, winter sets in.

Time is unmoving, and death impends
Coldly we are grasped, darkness descends.
The hope of the youthful is dashed,
And ancient moods are present.
Old spirits take the field,
waging harsh warfare in dusky glens.
Their biting blades cutting and cracking
Cruelly shaped axes mercilessly hacking
And the wind always blows.

And so it is with the soul's wintry blight,
Heart tightly bound in clenched knuckles of white.
The wail of the wretched is sought,
And pity cannot be mustered.
Old hatreds rally round,
to buttress sore envy and bitter grudge.
This sorrowed vein, numbing and chilling
Shadow'd distemper, rending and killing
And the wind always blows.

The Eighth Tale

The Right Hand Path

Chapter 16
Prototype

Prosthetic

A doll sat on the shelf and cried,
Unasked for gift held deep inside.
Flawed, she fell from off the shelf,
more true to life than life itself.
Cog and gear, a pulley push,
ball and socket twist.
Synapse fire and circuit close
from ankle, hip and wrist.
Grinding in both joint and soul,
Forever grasping for control,
A raw revenge is now her goal
For all the love she's missed.

TOBI WAS loading a bag into the back of Dr. Galen's car when he heard a voice behind him.

"Yo."

He turned to see Anomalie standing in the driveway behind him.

"Yo," he said, under his breath. He wasn't sure how to respond, Anomalie had been speaking more to him lately, including him in her comments and small jokes. He had been watching her from afar as she'd practiced with her new leg, learning how to walk slowly and then to run with an ambling gait across the yard. But, he still felt bad when she spoke directly to him, especially when the others weren't nearby to deflect the tension that was between them. "How da leg feelin'?" he added.

"Better," she said, walking closer to the rear of the car. "What's in the bag?"

"Just gear. I got spots in the city. Find tech and stuff for Engineer. So yo neh,"

"So yo neh," she returned, without looking at him. After a pause, she spoke again. "Can I go into the city with you this time?" she asked.

Startled, he stopped what he was doing. He wagged his head up and down, nodding. "Yea, believe it!" he exclaimed. "Anytime 'Nomalie. Just ask."

"Well, I'm asking now," she said. "Doc Galen says that there are clubs in the city. Music clubs, where they have bands and stuff. You know what I mean?"

"Like Burst-style or Lambda? Like from home? No way..." he started, but she cut him off.

"No, not Burst. Like old-school stuff. Like from this time. Punk-rock and thrash, stuff like that. With real guitars," she said, looking at his face to see if he understood.

He considered it, trying to recall. "Yea. I know it. Vintage rokkers on stage, neh? I seen a few spots," he said. "I can take you."

She smiled and reached out to muss his spiky hair, and he smiled in return. "Really? Cool. Thanks, Tobi." She started to turn away.

"No problem, 'Nomalie. We goin' soon, though." He swung the car's hatch shut.

"Yea, I'll be here," she said over her shoulder.

"And 'Nomalie…" he said quickly. She stopped. "I really sorry."

She didn't look back. "I know you are, Tobi," she said, and walked inside.

THE DRIVE INTO THE CITY only took about an hour; Tobi sat in the back seat and slept, his mouth hanging open, intermittently snoring. Anomalie was too excited to sleep; Dr. Galen drove while she sat in the passenger seat and craned her neck to stare out the windows. The scenery changed gradually, from countryside to low buildings and shops, dotted by houses, to taller and taller buildings and finally, to a huge urban sprawl, cris-crossed with wide freeways and train lines. It was just beginning to get dark, the sun setting at the end of a long avenue, straddled on both sides by skyscrapers, when Dr. Galen pulled the car to the side and shifted it into park.

"This is where I leave you two," he said. "Tobi already has a phone but I'm giving you another." He reached into a pocket, pulled out a small flip phone and handed it to Anomalie. She held it in her hand, but appeared to be puzzled by its function. She turned it this way and that, examining it. The doctor laughed. "Too low brow for you I'm sure." He took it back from her and flipped it open. "Tobi did the same thing when I gave one to him. Look, it's simple. My number is pre-programmed into it. Just hit this button..." He did it, "and...*voilà!* My phone rings. Call me when you two need to be picked up. I'll meet you back at this corner when you're done. Got it?" She nodded at him, took the phone back and shoved it in a pocket. "And here. Money to get in." He handed her some folded bills. She smiled in thanks and slid the money into another pocket. Bleary-eyed, Tobi was coming back to consciousness in the back seat; Anomalie stepped out of the car and waited for him to join her on the sidewalk. He went to the back of the car and removed his tool-bag, shoving it into his backpack. Dr. Galen waved goodbye to both of them and pulled the car away and into traffic.

Night had truly fallen on the city by now and, as they stepped off down the sidewalk, Anomalie was dazzled by the sparkling lights of the city as the nightlife came awake. The city seemed to take on a different rhythm as new people replaced the old; the day workers made their way out or to their homes and other, fresher walkers filled the sidewalks and streets. Anomalie took it all in, watching small packs of people make their way to nighttime haunts. In the midst of the moving crowd, she started to notice an emerging pattern; she saw a type, a younger, more vibrant group, dressed in hoodies and baggy pants, walking and riding skateboards, moving against the crowd, and she could feel them converging on a central target. She felt the pull as well; she wanted to see where they were going. She and Tobi turned onto a street off of the main avenue and she saw a crowd of kids and older people, dressed like the kids, swarming around a single door.

"That da place. Up there," said Tobi, pointing. "Asylum. I always see punk rokkers outside."

Anomalie felt her heart jump into her throat. She wanted to hurry ahead of Tobi, to get into the crowd and chill, mingling with the other kids. She couldn't believe that it was real. A punk club. With punk kids outside, waiting to get in. For years, she had scavenged old artifacts from this period, from this very place. Old bootleg tapes and vids from Asylum were cherished parts of her collection. She had copies of copies of fanzines, showing black and white snapshots of bands on stage here. She would lay for hours on her mattress in the Old Zone and try to imagine what it must have been like to be on the stage, or even in the crowd here. And now it was only a half a block away.

"C'mon Tobi. Let's go, the line's not that long." she said, hurrying him along.

"Don't stress 'Nomalie, they not goin' anywhere." he answered, but he hurried anyway. They passed through the crowd of kids, some sitting on skateboards on the curb, some smoking and laughing, and found a place in line. Anomalie tried to look cynical and bored as she leaned against the brick, but she was sweating in anticipation. Tobi bummed a smoke from a kid passing by and lit it.

"You happy 'Nomalie? This place cool?" he asked, between drags.

"Yea, Tobi…it's cool. Thanks. For bringing me," she answered and then looked ahead; the line was moving.

They reached the door and saw the girl who was taking money, her arms were completely covered in old-school tattoos, seated next to her was a skinny guy with a hand-stamp. There was also a large, muscular skinhead, standing to the side of the door, his arms folded and a mean look on his face. Anomalie quickly figured out the system. She fished into her pocket and dug out the bills that Doc Galen had given her and separated out a twenty.

"For me and him," she said, gesturing to Tobi. The girl took her money and stuffed it into a cash drawer. She held out her hand and the skinny kid rolled the hand-stamp across the back of it. Tobi did the same. As they turned to walk in, the skinhead unfolded his arms and stopped Tobi.

"Hey son, how old are you?" he said. Anomalie's heart caught in her throat. Tobi definitely looked too young for a club like this.

"I thirteen, yo neh. How old *you*, son?" shot back Tobi. He lifted his goggles and glared belligerently up at the skinhead.

The skinhead laughed and refolded his arms, waving them inside with a twist of his head. Anomalie breathed a sigh of relief and they were inside.

Inside, the club was dark and they walked down a long hall where the walls were covered with scrawls of graffiti and stickers. Anomalie tried to pick up some of the things that were written there but there were too many for her to focus on just one at a time. There were various people leaning against the walls, talking and hanging out. They stepped into a larger room and she saw the stage at the far side. There were kids sitting along the edge of the knee-high stage and walking back and forth between microphone stands and assorted drums and amplifiers. She couldn't see a difference between the roadies, the band or the fans; there was a relaxed party atmosphere that was totally new to Anomalie. She and Tobi moved to a spot near the front of the stage and took it in. They watched the stage setup and the kids in the crowd, and couldn't decide which was more interesting. There were kids writing tags high up on one wall with fat, metallic markers, their friends holding them by their legs so they could make their mark higher. Two kids were in the middle of the dance floor slap-boxing as their friends watched, laughing.

Anomalie was startled by someone tapping her on her shoulder. She turned to see a boy about her age with a huge bag slung over his shoulder. In his hand was a paper flyer.

"Here," he said. "You should go. It's next week."

She looked down at the flyer and saw another show, at another club, being advertised. She looked back up at the kid. "Maybe..." she said awkwardly.

"I drum for this band," the kid said, pointing at one of the bands on the flyer. "We need as many cool people to come as possible 'cause its a benefit show."

"Okay," she answered, not knowing what else to say.

"Plus, you got cool ink," he said, pointing to the ink collar tattooed on her neck. Tobi gave the kid a frown and the kid started to walk away. "Laters," he said.

"Yea, laters," said Tobi, throwing a dirty look at the kid's back. Anomalie looked at Tobi in surprise and then snorted, laughing.

"Thanks for the save," she said sarcastically.

"Psss," he said, still frowning at the retreating kid. "Cool ink. So yo neh."

Suddenly, and loudly, the drummer on stage started his sound check. First, he pounded on the snare, then the kick drum and toms. When he finished, the bass player stepped out from where he had been connecting cables on his amp and slung his bass over his shoulder. Kids started to congregate near the front of the stage; when the guitar player walked out, a short rush of applause and a howl rose from the gathering crowd. One of the roadies hurried across the stage in a crouch, running a mic cable from one side to the other. Then, he pulled out a roll of silver tape and started taping cables to the floor. By now, there was a tightly packed crowd filling in the area in front of the stage. Anomalie and Tobi were beginning to be pushed away and jostled, so Tobi hopped up onto the stage, holding a hand out to her. She wasn't sure if they would be allowed up there, but she looked across to the other side and saw more people climbing onto the stage, some carrying large old fashioned cameras with flash attachments. She took Tobi's hand and he pulled her up just in time. She looked back to the dance floor and saw that it was completely jammed with people. She and Tobi found a small spot in between some other kids and looked toward the center of the stage.

A kid who looked to be a few years older than Anomalie came from where he had been standing on the far side of the stage and ran out to where a microphone stand had been placed in the center of the musicians. He was dressed in cut-off camouflage shorts and sneakers, with a hooded sweatshirt. He had a cap with the brim turned backwards on his head. When he reached the mic stand, he pulled the mic off and unwrapped the cable from the stand. The crowd erupted in a deafening roar, hands held above their heads. Anomalie looked from her vantage point to the first few rows of spectators and saw a sea of smiles. She smiled too. A kid that was standing next to her ran out to the edge of the stage and rolled off onto the people in the front row. Laughing, they held him up and pushed him to the other side of the crowd. He rolled off of their hands and back onto the stage. No sooner had his feet touched the floor again then he boosted himself backward into the crowd. This time they caught him but he ended up rolling off further back into the crowd.

The kid who was holding the mic held it to his mouth and shouted, "What's up, Asylum?" There was another roar from the crowd. "We're Strait Jacket, from upstate. This song is called 'Soul Culture'"

The drummer raised his sticks above his head, looked over to the where the guitar player was waiting for a cue and slammed his sticks down toward his cymbals. To Anomalie, it was like a riot erupted. The three band members standing on the stage: singer, guitar, and bass, leaped into the air as if they were performing a snowboard trick but without the snow or snowboard. For a slow second, Anomalie saw them in the air and it was exactly like the snapshots she had seen in her old, yellowed magazines. Then the music burst from the amplifiers, the singer started singing and the crowd started dancing. She was happier than she had ever been in her life.

There were two other bands that played that night, 'The Action Figures' and 'Danger Close'. In between sets, Anomalie and Tobi met people from different places, some from different countries, with different ages and ideas. They wore different clothes and had different hair, there was no reliable way to categorize the various groups that filled the club. It was a paella of cultures, each ingredient lending a flavor to the mix but never losing its individual identity. It was all a happy blur to Anomalie.

As they were watching the final band about to start their last song, Anomalie felt a tug at the hem of her pants. She looked down from her spot on the stage and saw a young woman's face, looking up at her from beneath the folds of a hood. The woman motioned to her to get down from the stage; she did and tugged Tobi down with her.

The three of them stood together while the band wrapped up its set. After the last song, the lights in the club came on and the crowd started to spread out.

"I saw you on the stage. I wanted to talk to you," began the woman. She was only slightly taller than Anomalie, dressed in a loose, hooded top and leggings, all of a dull, bluish, slate color. Anomalie could tell that the woman was strong. When she shifted her weight, Anomalie saw lithe dancer's muscles ripple beneath her leggings. She kept her hood pulled closely to her face, near her eyebrows; Anomalie couldn't discern the details of her face.

"I know that you're both augmented," the woman said.

They both stared at her. Tobi stepped in front of Anomalie, between the two of them. "How you know that?" he demanded.

"Look, I know this sounds shocking," began the woman, "But I am too. I've been scanning you since you came into the club."

Anomalie grimaced in annoyance. If their implants had been fully functional, they both would have realized that someone else had been scoping them. "What do you want?" she asked.

"I'm not your enemy. Far from it. I know Sigil."

At the mention of Sigil's name, Anomalie frowned, her eyebrows lowering. "How? How do you know him? From where?"

"Do you want to go to a better place, quieter? We can talk more there. It's not far," asked the woman.

Anomalie looked at Tobi; he shrugged. "We got time. I usually out way later," he said.

Anomalie nodded at the woman. "Sure. Lead the way."

They made their way through the dispersing crowd and back out onto the darkened street. Small groups of kids drifted up and down the sidewalk, moving to the next club or party or home.

As the three of them walked away from the club, Anomalie attempted to find out more.

"I'm Anomalie, this is my friend, Tobi," she offered.

"I'm the point," the woman spoke in a low voice.

She adjusted her hood, burying even more of her face in shadow. "I was told that there would be some from the Potential era arriving soon. We didn't think that it would be this soon. But time travel has a way of screwing up your schedule, I guess. Is Engineer with you?" she asked.

Tobi was about to speak, but Anomalie cut him off quickly.

"Why should we trust you? You won't even give us your real name. What's your deal? Are you from the grids too? How did you get working 'plants here?" She looked at the point suspiciously.

"I understand why you find it hard to believe, but you have to admit, a lot of this is unbelievable right?" Anomalie had to agree with that, the point went on. "My implants are not as advanced as yours or Engineer's or even Tobi's. . ."

"Oi!" interrupted Tobi, giving her a sharp look.

"No offense meant. I only mean that my implants were designed in this era. I'm one of the first prototypes of the Judicial implanting protocol. Compared to what you two are carrying, my gear is positively primitive. But it has the benefit of working with the current network. As small as that network is."

When the point mentioned Judicials, Anomalie realized something odd. She hadn't seen any Judicial Troopers or vehicles or any Judicial presence at all once they were near Asylum. There had been some on the highway as they approached the city, Anomalie had marveled at their vintage design, but she hadn't seen any in the vicinity of the club. The existence of the club itself was strange, everything that Anomalie had learned in school, all the facts relating to this time period had described it as a cultural wasteland. According to her history classes, clubs like Asylum had been shut down by this point in the Judicial Rising. But, Tobi hadn't batted an eye when she had asked him about it, he had immediately told her that he had seen places like it. She was about to ask the point for an explanation, but before she could, they arrived at their destination.

They had covered only a few blocks when the point stopped in front of a fence that was covered by tattered construction screening. The fence extended the complete length of one city block, obscuring the view of what lay inside. The point led them to a far corner, where the light from the streetlights was blocked by some overhanging scaffolding. She looked in both directions, up and down the sidewalk. The street was silent, abandoned.

"Quickly now. Over the fence," she ordered, and began to climb. "The barbed wire is loose here."

Anomalie quickly shot a glance toward the way they had come, but there was no movement. She moved toward the fence but Tobi stopped her, motioning to her leg. She brushed him off. She knew that he would use his implants to assist him over the fence, as would anyone from her era. But she was used to working with joints that had imperfect assists or none at all. She could climb a fence with only her arms if she had to. Tobi watched in admiration as she climbed behind the point, who was already at the top, holding the curls of barbed wire aside for her. She passed through the wire and started climbing down on the far side. When she reached the bottom, she looked up to see the point holding the wire for Tobi as well. The point saw that they were both safely down, then carefully put the wire back into place and dropped down next to them.

"What is this place?" asked Anomalie, looking around at the shadows of a ruined and collapsed building.

The point motioned to them to follow her as she started to walk to the crumbled walls of the wrecked building. In a quiet, midnight voice she said, "This is where they fell from heaven."

Chapter 17
The Recurring Dream

*Of a dark ritual
and of a narrow escape*

"SO THIS is where the Abbey of St. Dismas stood?" said Anomalie softly. "Why did you bring us here?"

The point led them along one of the crumbled outer walls of the monastery garden, and through a large hole broken in it. The massive, granite stones were covered with thick moss and ivy clung to the sections that were still standing.

"I was here when it fell," she said, running her hand lazily along one of the cornerstones without looking behind her. "With Sigil and Mara. I helped them to get out." Then she turned and looked directly into Anomalie's eyes. "I helped them find *you*."

Anomalie looked at the shattered foundation of the building, filled with pieces of rubble the size of small cars. How could anyone survive such a thing?

"Who are you, really?" she asked, an edge creeping into her voice. There was something unearthly about the ruins of the Abbey, a floating sense of eeriness that was beginning to grip her. She saw that Tobi sensed it as well, he kept far away from the point, edging along the inside of the wall with his back to it. Anomalie looked at the point more closely, she could barely see her face under her hood and it had been dark in the club when they had first met. Now, in the moonlight and at a slight distance, there was something familiar about her. Perhaps in her voice, or in her way of standing; Anomalie was certain that she had seen this woman before.

But it was impossible, she had been nowhere but Mara's house since they shifted to this era. She had actually been unconscious until two weeks ago, and the only people that she had seen since then had been Mara's mother, Dr. Galen, and her friends. She stopped dead and reached out her hand to stop Tobi.

"You *followed* us. You *are* from our era. Did the Monarchy send you? To kill us? To kill Mara?" Her voice was starting to rise both in volume and intensity, but before she could say any more, the point spun and clamped her hand down over her mouth. Her movement had been so swift that neither Anomalie nor Tobi had been able to react. One moment, she was yards away and the next, she was between them both.

"Be quiet! Both of you. I said before, I am not your enemy. But this place is no longer a sanctuary. Instead it is a nest of vipers." She angrily released Anomalie, and stood still before her. "You must believe me. I sought you out to warn you."

Anomalie tried again to look more closely at the face that was hidden in the shadows of the hood, but recognition still eluded her. "If you're not from our era, then why do you seem familiar to me? And if this place is so filled with vipers, why bring us here?" she shot back at the point, irritated that she had been gagged so easily.

"Come, both of you. Closer to me," said the point, motioning to them to sit on a low wall near where she stood. When they had, she lowered herself to sit on a stone facing them. "This place, this crumbled church. It is not what it seems," she said in a quiet voice. "When they laid the first stones for it, I was a child, many, many years ago. My own father was one of the masons who labored on its building. Many of them died to conceal the secret of how it was constructed." She paused, considering her words. "And to conceal the contracts that were made and sealed inside the stones."

Tobi was silent, but Anomalie spoke up. "Contracts? What are you talking about?" She was beginning to believe what the point was saying but still couldn't understand.

The point continued patiently, "Anomalie, just listen to what I say. These beings, Angel, Faerie, Archon. They have business beyond what we humans can know. Dealings among themselves that we are not privy to. And often, the payment that they demand is wicked indeed." She lifted her head to see their faces, still concealing her eyes below her hood. "Often, they demand sacrifice."

Anomalie was starting to comprehend what she was hearing. In her way, she had understood that Mara and Sigil were profoundly different than anything that she had ever imagined. She had believed Sigil when he explained that he had fallen. Far in the back of her mind, she had understood that he had committed a great crime. But, it had felt so far beyond her, so alien and strange that she hadn't really questioned any of it. The great power that she had witnessed, that she had wielded herself with Sabaoth, had made her so energized and hopeful, she had never really considered what it may have cost.

"You mean *human* sacrifice?" she said slowly.

"That, and worse," answered the point. "When Solomon and Mara were fostered here, I was a soldier, serving in a unit that Sigil had deployed. I had twisted and forced my fate to get that posting. I did it so that I could return here when it fell. The Culture War had only just begun, but I knew that one of the first targets of the Monarchy was to be this Abbey. I knew that Sigil would be here on that day. I knew that he would try to stop them. And I knew that I had to insure that he did it."

"But, how...why...?" stammered Anomalie, trying to fit together pieces of what she'd seen. "How could you even know all this? Who are they to you?"

The point got to her feet in front of them before she spoke. "I know this because, when this Abbey was commissioned by them, *I* was to be their first payment."

Anomalie only thought for a moment before she stood up, pulling Tobi to his feet. "I got it. I mean, I got as much of it as I need to get. And they wanted to do the same to Mara, right?"

"Yes," answered the point. "The destruction of this Abbey was a ruse. It is still being used, in plain sight of the city."

Anomalie looked doubtfully at the rubble of stones strewn around her. The point saw her expression. "I can show you," she said.

Anomalie swallowed, patted Tobi on the shoulder and set her jaw firmly. "Let's go," she said.

The point led them to a dark alcove hidden near one of the corners of the garden wall. "There are tunnels, far below the Abbey. I've seen and scouted them before. This is the entrance. The Judicials have no idea that it has been compromised. We can enter here," she said.

Anomalie nodded and followed her as she pushed herself through the narrow opening. Tobi nervously entered behind them. They made their way along the initial tunnel, and then it opened up and the floor became a series of descending ramps.

"They use this passageway to bring supplies down to the lower level. It branches off to a wider tunnel here," said the point as they passed the branch. "It will be more closely guarded further on. We must be quiet and careful."

Both Anomalie and Tobi nodded and moved stealthily behind her. They were both accustomed to sneaking past Judicials, but both were also without the extra senses that their implants gave them. They moved as if it was their first time infiltrating. Once, Tobi kicked a stone and it skittered ahead of them through the tunnel. The point looked back and glared angrily at him. They froze, but after a few nerve wracking seconds, they relaxed slightly and moved on.

They finally reached a smaller tunnel that led to the left of the main passage and the point led them down it. It curved slightly and opened into a small, tight room, the ceiling only a bit more than head height. There was a tiny slit of a window near the top of one wall; they could see flickering light coming through it.

All three of them went to the edges of the slit and peered through. They could see into another chamber where a number of Judicial troopers and officers were seated around a low, stone table. Around the edges, the table was covered in Angelic script, near the center were other characters carved into the stone. Anomalie thought that they might be Chinese, but when she looked more closely, the symbols seemed to swim in front of her eyes and change.

She looked back at the point and nodded, as if to show her that she believed her, but the point twitched her head back to the window to direct Anomalie's attention there. She looked, and was shocked to see three woolen-robed priests enter the chamber. They made the now familiar sign that she had seen Mara and Sigil make at the cathedral in the Crax. The same sign that Brother Demen had returned to them.

The priests sat at the table at the three places that had been left to them and one priest, seated in the center, began to chant.

The Judicials picked up the chant from the priests and soon there was a low, sonorous hum reverberating through the chamber.

Anomalie silently edged closer to the point, whispering in her ear. "Okay, we've seen it. I believe you. We should go." The point nodded and started to back away from the window, motioning to the others to follow, but stopping suddenly. The sound from the chamber had increased in pitch and volume and their eyes were drawn back to the room. The symbols on the table were glowing softly but with increasing intensity. Then, it seemed as if they lifted up out of the stone where they had been carved and floated slightly above the table. The symbols began to spin around the edges of the table, the Angelic script in one direction, the strange, Asian script in the other. From the center, where the script had become a glowing blur, a hazy fog started to rise. The fog began to form into a shape both monstrous and inexplicable. The shape seemed to adhere to no natural, organic law. It was as if the creature were perhaps inside out, but had more than one or even two insides. Anomalie felt like she would vomit; she looked at Tobi and his eyes were spread wide in terror. At her neck, she felt the anchor tug angrily at its chain. "I'm serious," she hissed at the point. "Let's go. Now."

The point was already on her way back to the main passage. Anomalie and Tobi hurried behind her, trying as hard as possible to remain quiet in their agitated state. They had nearly made it back to the first turn when Anomalie fell. She crashed to the ground, loudly splaying her legs behind her. Tobi, who was rapidly advancing behind her, entangled himself and twisted, impacting the wall with a resounding clatter. For a brief heartbeat, Anomalie was at a loss for an explanation. Then, when she tried to stand, her heart dropped. It was her leg. She had been training and attending therapy sessions with Doc Galen everyday and she had felt confident. He had voiced some concerns to her about her stamina when walking on her new leg but had allowed her to go into the city with them. But now, she had pushed it too far. She tried again to stand, but it was no good. Her prosthetic had failed.

The point spun around to see Anomalie on the ground, Tobi leaning against the wall and lights moving from the bend in the passage beyond them. She began to run toward the two of them, just as a four-man Judicial fire-team came around the corner. The point leaped over Anomalie, using Tobi's shoulder to boost her distance, landing like a cat in the center of the passage. Anomalie barely had time to register in her mind what she saw next. The fire-team members were just lifting their weapons into their shoulders as the point slid past their leader. Then, she was among them. Anomalie was entranced as she saw the point move. She slipped under the muzzle of the next trooper's weapon and stood straight up. As she stood, the barrel of the rifle was on top of her shoulder. She spun slightly as he passed and she lifted her arm up and around the barrel, twisting against the trooper's wrist. The rifle was suddenly in her hands; she shifted back again and the trooper's rifle sling was wrapped around his neck, tightening. The point cranked it once and moved on to the next trooper. She dropped to the floor, her leg sweeping around and up into the back of his knees. Before he hit the ground, she had stood back up again but her leg had still not touched the ground. In a painfully beautiful pirouette, she swung her leg around and over her head, still spinning. Her leg crashed into the front of the trooper's helmet, increasing his rate of descent into the floor. She softly settled her leg to the ground and turned to the last two. The leader was closing on where Anomalie lay on the ground. The point raced the third man and nearly passed him, but instead, as he spun to catch up to where he had seen her last, she shifted behind him effortlessly and using both hands, pulled his head backward and down. His body hit the ground helmet first, but the angle of his neck was too extreme. There was a loud report in the tunnel as his neck cracked. The last man had stopped and was about to fire, he craned his neck to align his sights but Tobi hit him first. Tobi barreled into to the trooper at a full sprint, driving his shoulder into the man's gut. The rifle fired, but the round went high over Anomalie's head and down the tunnel. The trooper struggled with the young boy that was suddenly tangled in his gear, furiously swinging his fists at his respirator. He was about to dislodge Tobi with a heavy strike downward, but as his hands rose above his head, the point was behind him. She dragged a vicious looking boot knife across the trooper's throat, finding the soft spot between his neck armor and respirator.

She rushed to Anomalie as the trooper's last breaths gurgled from his throat behind her. "They will hear the shot," she said, with growing urgency. "You must go now. Quickly!" Anomalie tried once more to rise to her feet but slumped to the side again as the processors in her leg died. Immediately, Tobi was at her side. He bent down and wrapped his arm under her armpit, hefting her off the ground.

"I got her," he said. "Believe it."

The point nodded, and reached into a pocket. She pulled out a small canister and pulled the ring that was attached. She looked back down the tunnel to where the troopers lay and tossed it past them. It hit the ground, rolled, and started spewing out thick, white smoke.

She turned back to Anomalie, holding her by the shoulders and staring grimly into her eyes. In a desperate voice she said, "Hurry! Flee, Anomalie! And do not come back here. It is not safe. You must tell Sigil what you've seen."

"But he's dead," she answered. "Point. Sigil's dead." She hadn't wanted to tell her. At first, because she didn't trust her, but later, because she simply couldn't imagine a way. But now, she said it almost as if to quell her own fears with some sort of truth.

The point didn't pause. She shook Anomalie hard and made sure that she focused on her eyes. "No matter. Find him. And tell him what you've seen here." Then, she was gone in an instant, backing into and turning away in the rising smoke.

Tobi, holding Anomalie with his arm beneath her shoulder, turned and began to move as quickly as they could manage back toward the surface. They made first a right turn and then a left and entered a long, straight passage. Anomalie glanced quickly to both directions and realized that they hadn't come this way.

"This isn't the way," she whispered harshly. "You're getting us lost." She craned her head back and tried to pull Tobi but he didn't budge. "I said that this isn't the wa—"

"Look," said Tobi, pointing. She looked at where his finger aimed. Vaguely, through the dim light of the passageway, at the furthest end of the hall, she saw a portrait on the wall.

"Are you nuts?" she hissed angrily. "We have to go! So it's a picture. So what?" She tried to pull him again but, without her leg working, it was nothing but dead weight. He was able to pull her with him as he moved toward the painting.

"Look, 'Nomalie," he said, as they came closer to the portrait. "It's Point. Same chick as we just saw."

Anomalie was about to say something sarcastic but she saw that he was right. The same face that had caused her to think that the point was familiar to her was looking at her from the portrait. The girl in the portrait had a melancholy expression and seemed to look directly into Anomalie's brain. Before she could say anything, Tobi reached into a baggy pocket, removed a small knife, popped it open, and started to cut the painting out of the frame.

"Hey! What are you doing, you freak?" she exclaimed, as quietly as she could manage. "We have to go!" But Tobi finished cutting and pulled the canvas down. As he did, a parchment fell to the floor with it. Tobi deftly put the two together, rolled the canvas up and shoved it into his belt at the small of his back.

"We didn't steal nothin' tonight. Can't go home empty handed. Believe it," he replied. Anomalie shook her head, and they started back down the passageway.

They reached the surface level quickly, hearing shouts and a clamorous din behind them as they ran, Anomalie stumbling lamely with Tobi helping her along. When they pushed their way out of the tight opening in the garden wall, Anomalie was pressing frantically on the buttons on the phone Doc Galen had given her. In a low crouch, they made their way to the fence that they had climbed with the point and were up and over it in an instant, Tobi climbing first and and then pulling her toward him as she hauled herself up. Doc Galen picked up and, exhausted and out of breath, she furtively whispered into the phone, telling him where they were. Attempting to appear nonchalant, they hurried back toward a more populated part of the city. Before they made it back to the street that Asylum was on, Dr. Galen pulled up to the curb beside them.

Together, they got into the car and sat silently. Dr. Galen only looked at them each once before he nodded, put the car into gear and quietly drove them home.

Chapter 18

Creation

*Of the Faerie
and of Engineer's enlightenment*

A NOMALIE stormed into the garage, banging the door open and jolting Engineer awake. Tobi was close behind her, trying to catch up to steady her if she fell. She hobbled over to where Engineer was leaning over a workbench, littered with scraps of circuitry, and banged her crutch against the leg of his stool.

"Your tech sucks," she stated, a livid expression growing on her face. "We nearly got caught by Judies tonight, and god knows what else. This thing doesn't even work." She pointed down to where she was sticking her leg out for him to see. He bent over, wiping the back of his sleeve across his eyes, and looked more closely. He could see scorching at the seams of the upper casing of the prosthetic leg where the circuits had shorted. He frowned.

"Calm down, Anomalie," he said, without taking his eyes from the prosthetic. "Explain to me what happened. Exactly."

They both spoke to him at once, rushing to relate the story of the Abbey and what the point had shown them. Engineer held up his hand.

"Hold on…hold on! Okay. You, Tobi, go inside and fetch Dr. Galen. And you," he pointed at Anomalie. "Explain." As Tobi ran out of the garage, Anomalie told him what had happened to her beneath the Abbey.

"It just gave out. Then it got really hot and nearly burned me. What kind of wiring did you put into this thing?" She lifted her leg and Engineer reached down to pull it closer.

"Did you attempt to activate the Archon?" he asked as he inspected.

"No, I didn't even have time. The fight was over before I could even stand. You should have seen the point fight! It was amazin—" Engineer shushed her and pointed to the workbench.

"Hop up here. So I can remove the prosthetic." She did, with Engineer's help, and continued to chatter about their close call as he carefully detached her leg. After a few moments, he looked up from his work and turned to Anomalie.

"I don't see anything wrong with it. I just can't understand it. The tech looks good." He shook his head in frustration. Anomalie was about to respond when the door flew open and Tobi entered, followed by Dr. Galen and Mara.

"Doctor, could you come here and look at this please?" said Engineer. Dr. Galen nodded and joined him at the workbench. He adjusted his glasses and looked at where Engineer was pointing. He squinted and looked again, then he lifted his head and thought for a long moment.

"Anomalie, do you mind if I look at your leg again?" he asked. She nodded and cinched up her pants leg. Dr. Galen examined the raw end of the limb, then went to another bench to retrieve a magnifying glass. He returned to where Anomalie was sitting and, using the glass, reexamined her leg.

"Do you see it?" asked Engineer from where he sat.

"Yes…I see it…Very strange…" murmured the doctor.

"What is it?" asked Anomalie.

"Well…" began Dr. Galen. "It's rather hard to explain. Or even to understand really…"

"Just spit it out, Doc," she said, exasperated.

"There seem to be traces of material from the prosthetic embedded in some way into the new skin on your leg," he said.

"And there are traces of organic material in the main CPU of the prosthetic," added Engineer.

"Well, the prosthetic was rubbing me pretty raw, so that makes sense…" Anomalie said, looking back and forth between them.

"Yes, but the CPU is nowhere near the surface of the prosthetic. The organic material inside it can't be from you. Actually, it can't be from anywhere. The casing on the CPU was hermetically sealed. I just now opened it. It's contaminated with something, but nothing could have gotten inside. I'm at a loss," said Engineer.

"Engineer, can I take a look at the CPU?" asked Dr. Galen.

"Be my guest," replied Engineer.

Dr. Galen sat on one of the stools and peered into the CPU casing. He took some tools from his bag and scraped a small amount of material from the microprocessor and brought it under a microscope. He studied it intently for some moments.

"What do you think?" asked Engineer.

"It appears to have grown there. But it doesn't seem like any sort of material that I'm familiar with," said the doctor. "Some of the small formations seem spore-like, but crystalline in composition. Like silicon fungi. Yet..."

At the mention of fungi, Engineer's eyes lit up. He stood rapidly, knocking his stool to the ground. He moved quickly to the end of the workbench and returned to his original seat with a small bag of the mushrooms. He handed one to Dr. Galen.

"Does it look similar to this?" he asked. The doctor took a complete mushroom and was preparing to make a slide sample for the microscope when he was interrupted by Mara's small voice.

"Where did you find that?" she asked.

"Behind your house," said Engineer. He was focusing on Doctor Galen; he didn't look down at her. She spoke again.

"No. Not the mushroom. The *manna*. Inside the mushroom," she said. Engineer stared at her. Doctor Galen paused and turned to her.

"What did you say, Mara?" said Engineer. "What did you call it?"

"That's *manna*," answered Mara, pointing. "From fairies. They always have it."

Engineer slid quickly from the stool and crouched down next to Mara. He held one of the mushrooms out to her. "Can you show me?" he asked.

"Okay," she replied. She took her fingers and spread the gills of the mushroom apart. She dipped inside and when she pulled her hand back there was a thin film of bright, golden dust on the tips of her fingers. "This is *manna*," she said again. "The fairies leave it in some places."

Dr. Galen gave Engineer a quizzical look, seeking an explanation. Engineer obliged reluctantly.

"I've been trying to replicate some of the code that I had running in the Crax," he explained. "Without that kind of processing power available, I was forced to use some more exotic methods to stimulate my coding. I understand that shamans and other mystics used these methods during this era."

"You were taking mushrooms when you were designing the tech?" asked Dr. Galen incredulously.

"I thought that they would open my mind to a more divine perspective. I'm not the first to do so," said Engineer hotly. He was about to say more in his defense when Mara spoke again.

"You don't eat it *here*. That's stupid," she said, giggling. "Only where the fairies are. That's how they talk to you. There aren't fairies in here," she said, as if they were all foolish for considering such a thing. Engineer turned back to Mara.

"Do you mean that you can only eat the mushrooms where I found them?" he asked. She nodded.

"Then, if they like you, they'll come and talk to you," she said.

Engineer nodded slowly, coming gradually to understanding. "Of course. I get it. It's not the psychotropic in the mushrooms at all..." he trailed off. Then, he suddenly turned to Dr. Galen. "Can you compare just the...the...*manna* to the sample from the CPU, Doctor?"

"Sure," said Dr. Galen, motioning to Mara. She held out her hand to him and he removed a small amount of the shining dust from her fingers. He put it under his microscope and studied it carefully. "Yes," he said slowly. "It appears to be a similar composition," he concluded.

Engineer stood up triumphantly. "Then we should go back up the mountain. Back to where I found the 'shrooms."

"What, now?" asked Anomalie, "It's nearly midnight."

"Immediately," answered Engineer. "We've already been here in this era for too long. I need to figure this out."

He began to gather some equipment, stuffing it into his satchel and motioning to Tobi to assist him. When they were finished, he walked to the center of the room.

"Come, Mara. We have no time to waste," he said. Dr. Galen leaped to his feet.

"You can't be serious! You can't take her with you. It's the middle of the night!" he shouted.

"If she's going, I'm going," said Anomalie, pushing herself from the workbench and leaning unsteadily against it.

Engineer faced Dr. Galen with a fierce look in his eye. "I know you mean well, Doctor, but she is no ordinary child. She won't be in any danger, I assure you. And you," he said, turning to Anomalie, "you're in no condition to go."

"You can replace the CPU in that rig can't you?" she said, pointing to the prosthetic. "I can make it that far at least."

Engineer nodded and moved quickly to the workbench, but Dr. Galen was not dissuaded.

"You can't take them with you, Engineer. Anomalie is my patient and Mara is a child. I refuse to let them go with you." He took a step toward Engineer; Tobi stepped forward between them, his eyes challenging.

"Let them go, Michael." It was Mara's mothers voice. Dr. Galen turned to see her in the doorway. "He's right. Mara's not like an ordinary child."

Dr. Galen went to where she was standing and put his hand on her shoulder. He was about to protest when he saw a small tear welling in her eye.

"Emily…" he began, in a quiet voice. "Are you sure?" he finished uncertainly.

She nodded, her jaw set firmly as she tried to control her tears. She motioned for him to follow her outside the garage. Behind them, Engineer was rushing to replace the components in Anomalie's prosthetic. She waited until the doctor had stepped outside with her and then she closed the door behind them.

"She doesn't really belong here you know," she said. He nodded, understanding, but still visibly upset. "I believe that Anomalie will take care of her until all of this is finished." She stared up at the stars as they clustered above the hills behind the house. He put his arm around her and they walked to the middle of the yard, watching the stars together. A few moments later, Engineer, Tobi and Anomalie, with Mara's hand held tightly in hers, walked silently past them, slipping into the shadows of the trees.

ENGINEER AND TOBI crashed loudly through the brush, retracing their steps up the mountain. Anomalie and Mara followed closely behind, allowing Engineer with his flashlight to guide their steps. After only a few near misses, Engineer located the clearing where they had gathered the mushrooms. He waited until Anomalie and Mara caught up, and then he crouched down to speak to Mara.

"This is the place where I found them. What should I do now?"

Mara took his hand and led him into the center of the clearing; Anomalie and Tobi walked slowly behind them, both of them unnerved because of the deep silence of the woods. A bright, pale moon shone down into the clearing, casting long shadows across it in rippled waves. Mara and Engineer reached the center and then Mara stopped and pointed downward.

"Here," she said. "They left that for you." She was pointing at another cluster of mushrooms. Engineer squatted down and plucked a few. Gold flecks glinted on the underside.

"For me?" he asked. "How do you know?"

"They only come when they want something, someone to talk to," she explained. "I don't need manna. But you found it. They want to talk to you."

He held the mushrooms up to his mouth, hesitating, looking at her for confirmation. She blinked and bowed her head to him, and he chewed on them and swallowed. She backed away from him, joining Tobi and Anomalie at the edge of the glade and he lowered himself to a cross-legged position in the grass. He waited.

At first, he thought that the mushrooms were taking too long or that he hadn't eaten enough. He was about to reach down for another cluster when he realized that they were already affecting him; they had been since the moment they had touched his lips. Before, when he had eaten the mushrooms, the effects were in his mind, cerebral. There had been a shifting of consciousness, marked by strange movement and changes in depth perception. Now, there was only stillness. There had also been, the last time, an altered sense of his relation to nature, he had felt as though he understood natural phenomenon more deeply, identified with it.

But he hadn't been outside, he had been in his makeshift workshop, listening to music and struggling to understand computer code and equations. Now, in this glade, beneath the drifting moon, surrounded by swaying trees atop a hill, he had a powerful loss of understanding. He was awash in the vast distances of the space separating himself from the stars above and below him as he realized his actual position relative to them. He felt alone.

Then, they came to him. Softly glowing figures moved toward him from between the trees, converging on him as he sat in the grass. From somewhere deeper inside of him than his conscious mind, there arose music. And from within the music, he heard voices, speaking as one.

"You are the one known as Engineer. But, that is not your true name."

He recognized that it was not a question, but perhaps part of some greater ritual. He tried to speak but couldn't. He slowly let breath out of his lungs to calm himself, but instead, he became more agitated. He tried rather to simply think a response, to only formulate his words in his mind, but that didn't work either. From someplace in the center of his stomach, his reply suddenly came. Silently, he felt the words form inside him.

"I am Engineer now," he felt. *"My only name now."*

"This is so," sang the voices. *"You are. You have eaten our offering, in our sacred place. Now, we would speak to you."*

He felt surrounded by the glowing figures, hemmed in. He thought for a moment that he felt sweat beading on his forehead and trickling down his ribs beneath his shirt, but then he realized that he couldn't. He was entirely away from his body and the sensation of discomfort was only a vestige of his memories of his physical self. He felt panicked thoughts arising and fought for control, but there was nothing to fight with. So, he stayed still. The voices had waited for his stillness and spoke again.

"Why have you tried to learn our art?" they sang.

Before he could control it, again from the pit of his stomach, his reply formed.

"I could not know if what I was experiencing was real any longer or if it was just a dream. I knew that this *world was a nightmare."*

There was a pause, as though the voices were considering his response. Then,

"You have a story. Tell us," the voices sang.

And, bubbling up from deep within him, came his answer.

"I spent so many years in frustrated research, never quite sure even what answer I was seeking. I could not even verbalize a question. I simply felt, intuitively, that there was something much

greater than this life and no teaching addressed it. Why should it be so hard to grasp, so impossible to find? It made no sense. Did God not want us to evolve? Did he wish us to sit alone and scared in the darkness and shadow of human cruelty? There had to be a key that would release the deadbolt, some clue to the riddles that plagued the hopes of mankind. I promised myself that I would discover that key."

Another pause. The music changed; the voices seemed to confer together. Then,

"You have understood wrongly. But we will teach you our art. Be not afraid."

Engineer's mind collapsed into itself. He felt as if the crown of his head fell straight down through his body and into the earth below and past it. He fell with it. For a brief moment, it was as if he was empty, as though his very identity ceased to exist. Then, suddenly, the place that was empty was filled with a blinding light. He stared into it with his mind's eye, seeking the far edge of it but there was no ending. He felt like he was drifting in the light for an eternity and then, without warning, it ended. He was back in his body, drenched in sweat, sitting in the clearing. He nearly fell over in exhaustion but he reached out with his hand and steadied himself. He blinked his eyes and opened them. Still, all around him, were the drifting, glowing figures. They spoke, but now he could hear them with his ears.

"We have taught you. We have given you what you sought. Perhaps it is a gift, perhaps not."

He opened his mouth to speak but his voice croaked, brittle and dry. Finally, he managed to say, "Thank you."

"We will take Mara with us. You do not need her protection any longer," the voices said. He struggled to rise to his feet, comprehending what they had said. When he looked to his side, he saw Mara in the clearing with him. Anomalie and Tobi were just behind her, Anomalie reaching toward her with both hands. But, it was too late. The glowing figures wrapped around Mara like a cloak and lifted her gently into the air, away from Anomalie's grasp. Engineer heard Anomalie cry out in panic and saw Tobi tugging on her clothes to pull her back. When he staggered to his feet, the light was gone and Mara had vanished as well.

Chapter 19

Aftermath

T HEY WOKE up near the edge of the clearing, the early shafts of sunlight breaking through the morning mist. Anomalie had wept herself to sleep, with Tobi making feeble efforts to comfort her. Finally, after she fitfully dropped off, he had slept as well. Engineer had spent the hours contemplating what the visitors had shown him, trying to comprehend the staggering vision he had seen. When he heard Anomalie shifting awake, he moved closer to her.

"What are you going to do now?" he asked gently. She squinted into the fog as it burned off of the grass in the clearing and pulled herself upright, hugging her knees tightly to her chest.

"What do you think?" she answered plainly, "I'm going after her. And Sigil too." Tobi was slowly awakening; he yawned and rubbed his eyes, catching the tail of the conversation.

"Sigil?" he questioned, "He dedded. Believe it, 'Nomalie. We both seen it." Engineer remained silent.

"I don't have to believe it," she answered, a stoic look on her face. "I don't have to believe anything except what I want to believe. The point told me to find him, and I'm gonna do it." She rose to her feet. "And both of you are coming with me," she said with a note of finality.

Engineer stood up and followed her as she walked out into the clearing. They reached the center and stood at the spot where Mara had vanished. Anomalie stood looking up at the edge of the wide basin of hilltop where the sun was just rising above the trees. She looked quietly toward the direction where the fairies had disappeared. After a few moments of hesitation, Tobi walked out and joined them. They stood together, feeling the heat of the new sun warming the forest.

"Anomalie," began Engineer in a soft voice. "We...I don't know where to begin..."

"You got some sort of super intellect, Engineer. Use it!" she said firmly, cutting him off. "We begin at the beginning. Mara is gone because of you, because of Tobi, maybe because of all of us. But not because of her. She may be different, she may be powerful and strange, but in the end she's just a kid. And we're her only friends. So we're not gonna abandon her," her voice trembled slightly. "Her family let her go, tried to hurt her. So I'm not gonna let it go. Nobody's a nobody." Her voice regained its strength, "Nobody..."

She continued to stare into the mountains; Engineer looked first at her for a long moment, then he nodded and turned to face the same direction. Beside him, Tobi's eyes filled with determination as he thought about what she'd said; he set his jaw and, together, they faced the new dawn.

Chapter 20

Epilogue

ONCE AGAIN, the light of the sunrise crept beneath the door of the tavern as the story came to a close. This time, the mood was much more agitated. And again, the innkeeper was the first to speak.

"The young girl was taken again?" he exclaimed. The villagers murmured and began to shift about. It was clear that they didn't want the storyteller to stop, but the old man held up a hand.

"I've told you all the story that a single night can hold. I am in need of rest before I can complete the tale." He stood and started to move toward the stairs. The audience protested.

"But what of the machine girl?" said one villager.

"And the wicked boy who killed his own father?" said another.

The old man smiled and began to climb up to his room, waving off the complaints. But he paused when the one of the innkeeper's children raised her voice.

"But what happened to Corrina?" the girl asked in a small, timid voice.

The old man stopped climbing the stairs, turned back to the girl and sat down so that his face was closer to hers. "That is a good question, child. And perhaps the only one that truly matters." He rested his hand on her head and his expression softened. "I promise that I will tell that part of the story tomorrow." The little girl smiled and nodded. He ruffled her hair and stood again. He turned to face the villagers crowded around the foot of the stairs. "Once again, I thank you for your hospitality and for your gracious ears. Tomorrow, at last light, I will tell you all how it ends." And with that, he went to his room and closed the door.

-End Of Book Two-

Author's Notes

*Or, how we arrived at this state of things
and where it goes from here.*

MUCH HAS HAPPENED between the writing of Only-ness, the first book in this series, and the final draft of this book. I ran an anime and manga convention, went to college to study electrical engineering, traveled to Japan twice, wrote another album's worth of music and began to produce my own illustrations. I was distracted, busy, indifferent, bitter, depressed and a number of other excuses that kept me from writing this.

I worried about the reception of the books by the public and I feared a general lack of interest. I fretted over the complexity of the story and thought that readers might think I was trying to fit ten pounds of &*#?@! into a five pound sack. After all, the story shoved angels and demons, cyborgs, time-travel, punk-rock, fairies, military action and politics all into the same poetry laced narrative. To be completely honest, it's *weird*. I often considered leaving well enough alone, cutting my losses and forgetting about this story.

But there were a few reasons I kept coming back to it. A few, rather unrelated reasons, that eventually convinced me to muscle through the doubts. The first was a real belief in the characters. Sometimes a writer can actually begin to know the characters in a novel, to actually sense that the characters have this sort of independence of the writing, an agenda of their own that is made up of what they would do in situations other than the ones that they are thrown into in the book. Somewhere along the way, I began to really *like* the characters in these stories and to see facets of their identities that I wanted to see developed. I had no idea if anyone else would be interested, but I was interested enough to want to keep writing.

The second reason was my own situation in my personal life. There have been a few ups and downs for me in the past few years, many more downs than ups. If I've learned anything from that, it's that I really don't have much to lose if I don't keep creating. It's not so much about whether or not I have great success in life as an artist, it's just that I realized that without the creative outlet in my life, I don't much care about what's going on. If I chose not to create, I would perhaps have more success, but I would almost certainly hate my daily life.

The last, and perhaps most important, reason was the messages I got from readers, asking me when the next book would be out. The fact that someone other than myself is concerned about what's going to happen to Mara, or Anomalie, or Sigil, surprises and sometimes baffles me but, at the core, is greatly appreciated by me.

We live in an increasingly complex world, our time is perceived as our most valuable commodity and our time is whittled away by work, school, family, friends, health, politics and a wide variety of entertainments. Whenever someone decides to spend some of their time with a story and characters that I've created, I'm both honored and amazed. That, I think, was the major reason that I continued on with the series.

So, this one is for you, the rare person who got into it enough to reach out to me and ask for more. You make me feel like I'm not alone when I'm wrestling with writing, and hopefully I was able to pull something off that will make you smile and continue to cheer our heroes on.

Don't worry. The third book is in the works.

J.A. Wynn